Echoes c

M. L. Rayner

Echoes of Home
A Ghost Story

Illustrations by
M. L. Rayner

?

Question Mark Press

First published in 2020 by Question Mark Press

Copyright © 2020 by M. L. Rayner

Question Mark Press

Echoes Of Home/ M. L. Rayner. – 1st edition
ISBN: 9798553179045

Cover Design by: Emmy Ellis @ Studioenp

Echoes of Home

Prologue

The empty lands closed in around me. Alone and far from help, no one would hear my humble cries. It was the sensation of emptiness that caused my heart to tremble. An uncontrollable feeling. And a memory that would last a lifetime.

I was blind to it. And with no sight, came no sound. For a short while, remaining still appeared to be my only option. And for that brief moment, I waited impatiently for my vision to gradually adjust and desperately diminish the darkness that suffocated my senses. Distant shapes slowly hazed into view from a wall of nothingness. A faint yet questionable outline of an archway stood through the thick bleakness, though now becoming more visible and reassuring by the second. To the right of this, I was sure there would be a light switch.

Eagerly, I paced to the far side of the room, stumbling over a hollow metal object that lay hidden in my path. *A bucket maybe?* Its sound echoed through as it crashed rapidly across the darkened space, abruptly coming to a halt when smashing against the unknown.

Regaining my balance after such a surprising stumble, I lurched my clammy palm upwards, vigorously searching along the cold and stony surface. "Please…work," I muttered through tightly clenched teeth, as though repeating a desperate prayer. The unsettling tension never once swayed from the pit of my stomach as I silently looked to the ceiling.

At first, there was nothing. All remained as unnerving as before, including both hands that still remained tightly gripped upon the flick of the switch.

The bulb that hung directly above jolted intermittent sparks of life, steadily leading to a continuous warm glow. An invisible weight immediately lifted from my stiffened shoulders.

The area that only a moment ago portrayed so many secrets, now appeared to be nothing more than a former utility room. Not the most pleasant first impression of my new lodgings. The surroundings before me now appeared cramped and filthy, acquiring a strange sort of smell. A stale odour, similar to that of a stagnant pool that lay to fester. Odd… I hadn't recognised the stench when first stepping into the premises.

The contents it hoarded lay bare. A ceramic sink hung loosely from the wall, its tap suffering from an intermittent drip that over time would aid the current stench. A three-legged chair sat tilted on its damaged side, and beneath it, a paraffin can which caused my clumsy fall.

I wasn't at all fond of the room, it hid something - what, at this moment, I couldn't say. But despite the shine from above, there were hidden corners which the light did not touch. *The perfect place to watch*, I thought with an involuntary shudder. To my surprise, the door that led to the main body of the house was unlocked and opened smoothly with a firm twist of its handle.

A noticeable chill flew through the corridor that awaited me on the opposite side, its appearance gradually swallowed by the purest colour of the night. Another light switch desperately hung from its fixture, though after several attempts, the source provided nothing more than an unsatisfying click.

My footsteps echoed like a whisper from the ceiling above, and with each and every step, the placing of my feet became lighter as if not wanting to disturb any other occupants who might lurk within the house.

With each stride further ventured, the more the shimmering light from behind faded. I slid my sweating palms firmly across the withered wallpaper, its delicate pattern tearing instantly from the touch of my fingers. The hall soon came to an expected end, displaying two entrances that stood at either side. The first remained sturdily in place, unable to be budged from its swollen frame.

With only a slight urge to investigate, I attempted to gain access to the next room. As luck would have it, the door opened and I curiously peered inside. It appeared to be the main living area. And although my thoughts remained doubtful, it became immediately clear there was no issue in regards to the power supply in this room.

For the first time without worry, I entered and closed the door contently behind me. It was quite spacious at first glance and already cluttered with some fairly dated furnishings. I expected nothing more from this kind of dwelling. Not to my taste exactly, but I was more than happy to spend the night here and judge the remainder of the cottage when visibility was not at its worst.

A tall grandfather clock stood at the far end, and to my recollection correctly displayed the time of ten o'clock. Pulling my jacket sleeve over my wrist, I wiped the settled dust that clouded the clock's glass face.

A brown leather Chesterfield soon took my liking, its position directly opposite a beautiful open fireplace with logs either side just waiting to be burned. Thoughts of comfort filtered through my mind.

Nothing says home like a roaring fireplace, does it not? I thought to myself.

I dropped to my knees, placing the necessary wood onto the grate. It didn't take long at all before the fire was steadily burning, giving out the warmth and glow the room so desperately needed.

I climbed back to my feet and allowed myself to lifelessly fall backwards, knowing only too well the brown-cushioned chesterfield would safely break my fall.

Tiredness clouded my mind, and for the first time that evening, I felt content, as if hypnotised by the dancing flames of the blazing fire that stood before me. With heavy eyes, I sank my head back, and my mind wandered, never once considering that what I was about to witness would change my life forever.

Echoes of Home

Chapter One

I t was late January 2003. The cold weather had persisted and seemed to stretch annoyingly from October to May each year. As the first seasonal snow fell on the ground, children rushed to the streets showing wonderment and joy given they'd not experienced such weather over that Christmas period. Of course, at times they encouraged me to engage in their daytime activities of snow fights and sledding, to which I willingly obliged.

The snow lay thick that week. And as I stared out onto the front path during that first evening, the footprints of youngsters' play displayed boldly within the deep snow. With no let-up, it continued to fall from the lightless, cloudy sky.

I unlocked the door and stepped out onto the path. All was silent. Peaceful.

A deep breath of cool air speared my lungs, shortly followed by a sorrowful cry that came from behind me. My nerves startled with panic. As I abruptly exhaled, I turned, but no one was in sight. Not a soul. But the sound was clear. I ran inside, searching the rooms in desperate hope of finding the source of the noise.

But it was too late. By the time I reached her, the cries had already fallen silent.

*

I was born Leslie Wills, living at number twelve Brook Street. I was one of five children, and although it pains me to discuss my childhood life, it would be truthful of me to say we grew up in poverty – a miserable childhood some might call it. My parents struggled to put food on the table due to lack of money, and as much as I loved them both dearly, they failed to provide for all their children. My father drank away the family's income, blaming his addiction on the pressures of life, giving our mother more distress than necessary.

We lived in the city of Stoke-on-Trent. Our home, a small two-bedroom terrace house in the slightly populated area of Longton. Thirty-five years later, I'm still here. Not through my own choice, you understand, but due to unfortunate circumstances. Let's just say I never really felt I had the same chances as my older siblings. As we all got older, my brothers left the nest one by one, abandoning us younger children to cope with the broken family that remained.

By the time I was seventeen, I was the last child at home. My father died shortly thereafter from pneumonia, having been admitted to hospital for an overwhelming period of three months, leaving me to take care of my mother and the rest of the house. I worked steadily for fifteen years at Spode Pott Bank, one of the few remaining pottery works operating in town, trying my best to provide my mother with the care my father never could.

It was only a matter of time before my mother passed away also. Some form of heart attack apparently. She was here one minute and gone the next, lying ever so still, in an unpleasant facedown position, her hands still desperately clenching at her failed heart for relief. It was a sorrowful memory, with what I can only imagine to have been the worst pain imaginable. By the time I reached her, there was nothing I, nor anyone, could've done.

I arranged the funeral myself, trying desperately to get in contact with the brothers I felt I'd lost so many years ago, providing message after message, letter after letter with the most recent numbers and addresses I had to hand. To my disappointment, I received no replies in return.

As predicted, the weather was miserable on the day of the funeral. I remember it rained throughout on that cold February day, forcing whatever snow that remained to slowly melt to an unpleasant brown sludge on the ground. And, it's strange – it might simply have been my state of mind – but everything felt grey and gloomy, as if all the colours in the world had been wiped clean as the day sadly grieved for my mother's passing.

The funeral took place at St Andrew's. A small church just on the outskirts of town. After much consideration, I felt it was the best place for the service. The old Catholic building held many dear memories for my mother. Her marriage, the christenings of all five of her children, but also the funerals of her parents. *Yes, she would be happy to rest here.* And that gave me some peace of mind at least.

I walked inside the traditional church, immediately noticing that the building was in need of major repair work. It looked old, unused, and smelled strongly of damp that lingered in the air. I looked at the ceiling. A number of holes had been left unrepaired, allowing the rain to slowly leak through the roof and fall onto the stone tiled floor and wooden pews. Stilling at the front bench, I glanced back at some of the guests who had no choice but to sit apart in a desperate attempt to avoid the continuous dripping that came from above.

The service began, and the priest spoke those famous words I'm sure had just become a routine to him over the years, no matter how much he believed in his religion. Father Davidson had been with the church since I could remember. He was a frail old man now, probably in his late seventies, recognisable instantly because of his bright-purple nose, about which my brothers and I used to make unnecessary comments. Mostly to the effect that he was guzzling the church's wine stock. Obviously, our mother did not approve of our humour.

Father Davidson seemed nice enough, but he was ridiculously boring to listen to. In fact, his tone could put you to sleep if forced to listen to him for any length of time. Some part of me really wanted him to become intoxicated from the church's wine. At least it might've made the man a bit more interesting. Unsurprisingly, that never happened, but the thought put a smile on my face, if only for a brief moment.

To be honest, I couldn't remember a word that came from Father's mouth that day, my attention focused completely on the dripping rainwater that barely missed my feet as it fell from above.

He made several apologies during the service in regards to this, but reassured the gathered crowd it would be fixed to the highest standard come their next visit. I'm sure I thought the same as every other guest who sat nodding at the priest, purely to provide reassurance and put his mind at rest. But I had no desire to return.

My speech (if you could call it that) was short. I stood before the huddled crowd feeling each pair of eyes pressing me, hoping I would provide some form of emotional, heart-clenching statement. I despised talking in front of others, especially when they have expectations of what they wish to hear. After quickly clearing my throat, I said what was necessary, only showing my deepest appreciation to the sorrowful clump of guests who attended. Before I knew it, my awkwardness had reached its end. I swiftly exited from the altar and back to my uncomfortable seat.

It took a while for me to realise the church service had actually ended. The priest had walked away from the altar and already made his way toward the main doors. I stood sharply, trying at best to not gain too much attention from my ever-so-slow reaction and, glancing behind me, for the first time I realised there were actually very few guests who'd turned up for the service at all. Not that it wasn't to be expected. I had already envisioned it to be a small turnout. After all, my mother kept herself to herself. Not because she was a private person, you see, but purely because she felt the embarrassment of her life in poverty.

Looking back, I could always remember her shouting about the neighbours because of the attention her sons had garnered regarding their appearance and lifestyle. Yes, we didn't have a penny to our name at times, but the rest of the family accepted it, whereas my mother was a completely different matter. She always felt like she deserved more in life, and it didn't bother her to express it. Not to her children, her husband, nor anyone else for that matter.

I almost jogged across the small churchyard to what would soon be my mother's final resting place. The wind had really picked up, the rain even more unpleasant as it smashed against my face. After such a long time, the cold had really become uncomfortable. But it didn't matter, not at that moment.

As I watched the coffin being placed into the ground of the sad-looking churchyard, I felt a sigh of relief that this experience was finally at an end. Yet a deep, empty feeling came from within as I knew I would have to return to the empty home I wish I'd left all those years before.

As the burial came to a close, I thanked the priest for his kind words and shook his hand firmly. My mother was a true believer in religion and attended church regularly. So, in a way, I couldn't help but think the man whose hand I was shaking probably knew my mother better than I ever would.

I turned around, again showing my appreciation to the few guests who'd attended before making my way home. I don't know why, but I kept glancing through the small gathering of guests, hoping to find the only people I truly wanted to be there but had never showed – my brothers.

The journey home seemed to take longer than usual, and the rain remained consistent. It hadn't stopped since the previous night. And from the state of the sky, it didn't seem like it was going to stop any time soon. Arriving home, I stayed inside the car, not wanting to return unaccompanied to the empty house that once housed seven of us.

One of the neighbours stepped out from number ten. He was in a hurry, trying at best to avoid the open heavens. Walking past me, he stopped for a brief moment and looked at me kindly. Even though the poor gentleman was getting soaked to the bone from the aggressive weather, he acknowledged me with a nod. I returned the gesture instantly, and he continued to walk quickly on, probably not wanting to bother me due to the saddened circumstance.

I stepped out into the rain once again, sprinting up the council-slabbed path that now seemed completely flooded due to a collapsed drainpipe that ran alongside the group of houses. Struggling with my keys in a desperate rush, trying to refrain from getting even more wet didn't go according to plan. But, as usual, nothing ever does when you're in a hurry. I attempted to get the keys into the door a second time. That somehow didn't work out either. The keys slipped carelessly from my grasp, plummeting into a pool of grim water that had collected just to the side of the doorstep. Not really in the mood to start searching through the murky fluid, I remembered a spare key was always kept within the car. Sharply running back meant my shoes and trousers soaked right through as the rainwater rebounded with each and every step.

Chapter Two

By the time I returned to the door, my appearance must have portrayed a man at breaking point. I turned the key with shaking hands, finally entering the house, pausing for a brief moment, my heart pounding by the second. With my dripping wet coat placed on the rack, I rubbed my hands furiously, immediately locking the door behind me in the hope of losing the bitter chill that had surrounded me throughout the day.

"Right," I said to myself. "First things first."

I made my way upstairs to draw a bath, peeling off the clothes that stuck unpleasantly to my skin.

"It's over." I said with an instant sigh of relief.

I can honestly admit I felt a little better. The rain continued to bounce off my bedroom window, the sound dominating the upstairs of the house. But I was dry and warm. And for the first time that day, the rain seemed harmless.

I looked at my watch. The time was now five-fifteen p.m.

In the kitchen I waited impatiently for the water to boil. This would have been the first coffee of the day, which was impressive for someone who felt addicted to the stuff. I seemed to drink it morning, noon, and night.

As the kettle hissed and spat, a sharp knock struck the door.

I rolled my eyes at the thought of entertaining guests, and for a time I willingly ignored the short, loud knock, only for it to be followed by another. I had no intention at first to answer the call, but my guilty conscience soon got the better of me, and I remembered the aggressive weather that had struck me only a short time ago. With that in mind, I decided to greet the poor soul who probably stood like a drowned rat on the doorstep.

I walked down the hallway. The knock struck again, now much louder than before.

"Just a moment," I shouted in the hope the person on the opposite side would hear.

Unlocking both catches, I apologised for the person's unacceptable wait, only to find there was no one standing there at all. I was puzzled, standing unaccompanied in the doorway. The rain forced its way inside. Quickly calling to a young gentleman who was passing by, I enquired if he had witnessed anyone on my doorstep. The young man was kind enough to stop, allowing me to repeat the question as he held his hand up to cup his ear. The man looked vacant as he again glanced up and down the street confusingly, informing me of seeing no one at all.

Locking the door behind me once more, I stood in a flummoxed state, actually considering if it was even the door that had disturbed me at all. I took a few paces forward before stopping, half expecting to hear the heavy-handed knock once more. Instead, all stayed quiet.

Entering into the living area, I picked up newspapers and post that had been left on the floor some days prior. Curiosity soon took hold of me, and I sneakily tried to get a glimpse of the doorstep from the corner of the window. Or better still, get a glimpse of who may have been standing there just moments before. Of course, no one stood there. Nor did anyone stand in sight of the dismal-looking street.

I placed the items on the windowsill, only to be hypnotised by the rain smashing on the ground. I broke from my hypnotic state when I heard the water come to boil for the second time.

"Would you like a cup of tea?" I asked politely.

Obviously, I was answered by silence. I turned to the chair where my mother had always sat, only for it to now be empty. A chill shivered up my spine. It was an uncomfortable sensation, the thought of speaking to emptiness. The fact that the room stayed silent meant my surroundings felt even more uncomfortable. The chair had remained unused since my mother last rested on it. The tartan cushion now flattened from hours of use. I quickly moved from the room, my sight never leaving the chair. I didn't return to the living area that evening.

*

The next morning, I awoke dazed, followed by the worst persisting headache I had suffered in some years. I struggled to keep warm throughout the night, no doubt caused by the after-treatment of standing in the bitter cold the previous day.

Sitting up in bed, I looked outside, having to squint. The rain had stopped. The sun had risen and now beamed brightly through the uncleaned glass. My headache worsened.

Downstairs, the tormenting thought of talking to an empty chair the night before didn't seem to bother me so. The idea of feeling uncomfortable now seemed silly, childish even.

I suppose thoughts such as that only get you during the loneliness of the night?

I already decided not to do anything exhausting with my day, so I made my way into the living room and after falling on to the sofa, somehow felt exhausted from a full night's sleep.

I glanced around the room. All the pictures that hung uneven on the wall really seemed to bother me. It was hard to think I called this place home for the past thirty-five years. Now it appeared as nothing but an empty shell, with no memories left to be had. Sitting alone that day, I experienced utter hatred for my brothers who'd left me to look after the people they also called Mother and Father at one point in their life. Or was it just jealousy that angered me so? Never having the same opportunity to make something better of myself, as I'm sure each of them certainly had.

Chapter Three

As the days slowly passed, I felt manifestly worse regarding my predicament. Although my mother's irritating personality once bothered me, the true feeling of loneliness had already made its way into my life. My first shift back to work started that very morning. It came as no surprise that I didn't attend, giving my boss feeble excuses of feeling unwell. Instead, I spent the day on the sofa feeling sorry for myself. That day seemed to pass by in the blink of an eye. I received no visitors, which wasn't out of the ordinary. Nobody ever called – unless, of course, for religious matters.

In the evening, I received a phone call from what happened to be the funeral director. Thinking there may have been some form of problem with regards to their payment, I was pleasantly surprised to hear the voice of a young lady asking if I found everything satisfactory with the service they'd provided. We spoke for several minutes and, regardless of who it was, I found it nice to have the conversation, if only for a short time.

At seven-thirty, I reluctantly decided to have an early night. The house was silent, once again, as it had been for the past week. The only noises were the creaking of the floors and walls as the house settled once again for the evening. I felt myself slowly drift when my entire body jumped from the reaction of a loud noise.

"Is that the door?" I whispered to myself, my eyes widened in reaction.

I sat up waiting, wondering if I really did hear the noise that drilled sharply through my ears. Or was it just my subconscious mind, playing tricks on me furthermore? Quickly rising from my rested position, I staggered towards the upper window. Its view displayed the long street poorly in the dim light, but shortly, my eyes adjusted to the small, rectangular yards.

I peered down. Again, not a soul stood at the door. I got back into bed, now convinced my mind games were nothing but a result of tiredness.

Nothing more than trickery of the mind.

My head once again hit the pillow. To my knowledge, the rest of the night was silent and completely undisturbed by mind games of the heavy-handed knock.

*

I didn't want to feel this way any more. The next morning, I awoke and got dressed with what seemed to be the most positive attitude since my mother's passing. I didn't feel right, and if I didn't do anything about it soon, the sensation would surely worsen.

Before I knew it, I was out the door and quickly pacing down the street to pay a visit to the local family doctor. The surgery knew me rather well. *Too well, I suppose*, purely due to my mother's regular appointments for arthritis, brittle asthma, and blood pressure problems. Still, sitting in front of Dr Carson would always make you feel a little on edge. He presented himself like a good enough man but also came across as the sort that took great pride in looking down his nose at you when given the slightest opportunity.

Explaining my situation seemed difficult. Not wanting to come across as though I was going through some form of emotional distress, I informed him of recent events, which was easy enough, though it didn't take long before his expression was gradually lost.

"Depression." He waved off anything further I had to add.

"Depression?" I replied.

"Yes, depression. That's what I'm telling you. It's common enough for someone who's gone through an ordeal such as yourself. I'll give you some tablets that should help. Also, here…take one of these and make an appointment, all right?"

Carson handed me a small card, a faintly printed number in green ink on the rear. Clearly not a professionally printed card but more of an attempt to use the last of his remaining ink that drained from his office printer. I turned the card over, that displayed nothing. The doctor turned away from his monitor screen, again looking down the tunnel of his nose at me.

"You call them, and call them today…yes? I've seen you with your mother plenty of times. In fact, you're the only one I've seen with your mother. You took care of her…yes?"

I wasn't given the opportunity to reply before he continued.

"I knew your mother, you did well. And did what you needed to do. I'd go as far as to say you probably even took care of the entirety this past week…yes?"

Staring down at the card, I placed it into my right inner coat pocket.

The doctor continued to speak. "You call that number, and they'll see you. Mental health is not my knowledge-base," he suggested with the motion of his hand. "But I know a person who needs help when I see one. Get back home and make the appointment. I'm sure you'll feel better."

I was handed a prescription that listed medication to help me sleep, then quickly removed myself out of Dr Carson's sight. I can honestly say I didn't feel much better about the whole situation. I knew I felt depressed. So, having a man with a medical background tell me the exact same thing didn't leave me with much encouragement.

I walked back in the direction of home. The sun was hidden behind a single cloud, shifting the atmosphere into a kind of pre-storm dreariness as a slight breeze gently tossed the fallen leaves in an unorganised pattern across the footpath. I decided to take my time. I was in no rush, and I felt as though the fresh air made me feel a little better. Indeed, it awakened my senses.

I took a left turn off the side street to go through Queens Street, which kept my mind active. It was the busiest road in the area. Always people walking, jogging, gossiping. Still a rough area nonetheless.

I hadn't had breakfast so stopped by a local spot that was on my route, formally known as the *Pig Out* café.

I sat at the first available window table that looked out onto the busy road itself, taking out my mobile to occupy my time. I'd received an answerphone message from work. I played it, immediately turning the volume down just in case prying ears happened to overhear.

Hanging up the phone to return the call, I was immediately disturbed in the process.

"You order food?"

I nodded eagerly at the elderly owner. For now, the call could wait.

I have to admit the food went down a treat. And I happily washed it down with a strong filter coffee, peacefully watching the cars speed along the busy street. I retrieved the card given to me by the doctor.

Should I call?

I wouldn't even know what to say, where to begin, or how to explain. The local pharmacy would literally be a five-minute walk from here and was situated on the same road.

Finishing the coffee, I thanked the owner, who stood with elbows resting on the counter, casually reading his morning paper.

The pharmacy itself was unusually busy that morning. Patiently, I browsed the products that one would usually find only inside a pharmacy. Supplements I'd never heard of, let alone know what they'd be consumed for. Stinging Nettle, Marshmallow Root, Quercetin, Flower Pollen, Probiotics, Saw Palmetto, Uva Ursi, Pumpkin Seed Oil, the list went on. This stuff didn't look cheap either.

Who the hell bought all this stuff?

I could imagine some health freak somewhere knocking multiple tablets back daily, mentally convinced it would provide some form of benefit. But in fact, the pills would give nothing more than a placebo effect in return.

The medication was handed to me in a small paper bag. And, as usual, I was asked to confirm my address in front of the other listening strangers.

Here we go. I thought, as the words "Brook Street" were spoken over the counter. No one behind made a sound. They didn't have to. I knew what they'd be thinking, and in turn, what they probably thought of me. Brook Street had its reputation, just like any other town. Unfortunately, it was a reputation that seemed willing to be upheld. They were poor folks' houses, pure and simple. And built especially with that reason in mind. Families would come and go over the years. Yet, all fit the stereotypical resident the town had come to expect. Thievery, drugs, riots you name it, if it was Brook Street it happened. Despite it all, I never really cared. Well... not until a time such as this arose. With the queue now reaching the door, I left the building and continued the ever so steady walk home.

I happened to stroll around the area for much longer than intended that day, but eventually, the inevitable happened. My pace slowed when the sorrowful Brook Street came back into view. That empty feeling once again took over my body and thoughts. The house now felt like my own personal prison. A cell that I had longed to escape from, the desire growing stronger by the day.

Stepping through the door, I looked down the aged-decorated hallway. The light flickered before the door was firmly closed behind me, my jacket again slowly placed onto the coat rack. I wanted nothing more than to throw it back over my shoulders and walk out, though having nowhere to go other than pointlessly wander the town forced me in the position to stay.

I removed my shoes and placed them one by one on the rack then made my way down the small, narrow hallway, only to be greeted by a slow, whispering voice.

"Les?"

My neck hairs stood on end. My body jolted upright. And while I turned sharply in reaction to the low, smooth whisper, the living room door swung slightly ajar.

Echoes of Home

Chapter Four

The silence now became somewhat deafening. I waited, wondering if I'd in fact gone completely insane. Whether I really did hear a voice whisper my name was unclear at this precise moment. Yet, it seemed so real.

Frozen to the floor, I attempted to call out to whomever may have been standing in the room, although nothing vocalised. My voice had run away, leaving my terrified body behind. The only way of finding out who lurked inside the house was now left to actions alone.

Trembling on the spot, taking several deep breaths in order to calm my nerves, I placed my hesitant hand on the doorknob and slowly pushed forward. It remained unclear at first if anyone was present at all, but once the doorway was cleared, my sight became accustomed to the dim light. A tall figure stood in a long dark coat in the corner, its back facing me.

I was truly terrified to see that the figure did not react upon my entry.

I managed to gather words, demanding that the figure identified itself immediately. "Who the hell are you? How did you get in here?" My tone was more cowardly than intended.

The figure slowly turned around and looked straight at me, his saddened eyes gleaming through the darkness. I dropped to my knees instantly with disbelief and heartache. I shut my eyes tightly, pleading to awaken from what felt to be a rather vivid dream.

I gazed up toward the dark shadow once more, its features now so familiar to me. It really was true. My eldest brother, Jonathan, had come home.

"Come on, Les. Let's get you to your feet," the soft and somewhat comforting voice mumbled.

I stumbled upright. It took me a few seconds to understand the current situation. Allowing myself to fall onto the first chair available, I was soon joined by Jonathan, who sat opposite from where I so weakly rested. I placed my face into my hands, staring at the worn fraying carpet, struggling to get to grips with such a surprising visit.

An awkward silence filled the room that I broke with anger.

"I buried our mother, you know?" I didn't make any form of eye contact with him, and I couldn't tell you whether he did with me. But his response was slow in return.

"I know. I got your message," Jonathan replied promptly.

Not an ounce of sympathy was voiced from the eldest son. I avoided raising my voice in anger further, but it didn't work as well as I'd hoped.

"Great, good. Too busy to reply, then?" I yelled, the words increasing in volume. Tears quickly formed as my voice unwillingly crackled with uncontrollable emotion. I needn't have said any more, as Jonathan immediately held both hands in the air as if to surrender.

"I didn't come here for a standoff, Les, I don't have the time," his slow calming voice replied. "I didn't return the call because, to put it straight, I knew exactly how you'd react." Jonathan paused, perhaps half expecting me to voice my anger in response. "It's been twenty years since I walked out that door. I couldn't just show up and face a funeral."

I looked up and could tell Jonathan presented a look on his face of deepest sympathy and regret for me... But that didn't cut it. Not after all this time.

"I know how long ago it was, John. I never left." My words sprang out sharply. Wanting, no, needing to get my point across regarding this man's selfish actions.

Jonathan nodded as I spoke, agreeing with me almost instantly. "Exactly, Les. If you hadn't called me and left me those messages about the funeral, I would never have travelled through the night to get here, never would have known you were still here, for that matter. I thought you would have left as soon as you were old enough. Just like the rest of us did."

"I couldn't," I whispered softly. "I would have… But father died shortly after that. I couldn't leave our mother alone to look after herself, no matter how much I wished to leave."

Jonathan stood, taking steps towards me, placing his shaking hand on my shoulder.

"Les, I understand," he said, continually rubbing my shoulder. "You're a better man than any of us who left this place. We didn't think twice about looking back."

I placed my hand on his, almost forgetting the years of negative thoughts that raced through my mind about the brother who abandoned me twenty years ago.

I gazed down once again to the carpet and asked the question that rapidly wanted to slip from my lips. "Why come back, John?"

He sat back down on the chair opposite me, now never staring away from my line of sight. "I've come back for you."

Jonathan, although appearing like he'd done well for himself over the years, couldn't escape the fact he was exhausted, burnt out, and low. I would go as far to say the man needed a little help himself.

Soon after gaining my senses, I offered him a glass of whisky. The bottle had been kept under the kitchen sink for some time, and since our father passed, it had become a rare occasion for someone to indulge themselves in such a spirit. I poured him a double serving into our late father's round-bottomed whisky glass.

He sat in silence for a while, spinning the glass around his palms, the whisky swirling. "I'm in the property business." He still looked down at his untouched whisky.

I didn't respond to his small talk. To that he visibly shrugged and sat on the edge of the chair to speak again.

"Yes, property... I've done okay for myself with it, too, Les."

"I'm extremely happy for you." I hadn't been able to help the sarcastic tone that flew back harshly towards him.

Jonathan smirked, accepting the attitude with grace, still glancing at the glass that spun through his fingers. Again, the same awkward silence circulated the room before he broke the troublesome peace with the most unexpected question. A question without doubt, he would already have known the answer to.

"How much would you like to leave this place?"

At first, I wasn't sure if he was being serious or not. Again, I didn't reply.

He pulled some papers out of his pocket and separated them one by one on the coffee table just beyond my reach.

"There's a house, well, a cottage would be the correct term. A great distance from here. I bought it just short of five years ago, at auction, you see. And...well, to be honest, I've never really had a game plan of what to do with it. The house has remained empty for years."

Now paying attention to every word he said, I asked him bluntly, "Why not rent it out then?"

He took his time with a response, taking the first sip of the whisky from his glass. He sighed immediately after swallowing the throat-burning bourbon. Shaking his head, he then continued. "No good. Let's just say it's too far out for anyone to show any real interest." He leaned forward, over the coffee table, slowly unfolding the few bits of paper that were placed there. Picking the first one up, he reached over, passing it to me, before slouching right back into the chair and bringing the glass up to his lips for the second time.

I looked down at the wrinkled pieces of paper. The title read Elphin Cottage. I'd never heard of the address, but my attention was soon grabbed by what seemed to be the picture of the property. It was an enchanting stone cottage with two wooden benches situated directly below its windows and surrounded by land as far as you could see. In the distance stood an impressive mountain, its peak hidden by the cluster of clouds above.

I said nothing to Jonathan, though my facial expression would have indeed given away my interest. Instead, I read on.

Elphin Cottage - Situated in the small scattered hamlet of Elphin, in the North Western Highlands, this 1844 stone cottage nestles in uninterrupted views over the Sutherland mountain scenery of Sulliven, Cull Mhor.

Spacious living room, kitchen. Functional dining room, bathroom, utility room, upper landing, two double bedrooms and storage space.

I continued to read but was soon interrupted by the guest I forgot I had.

"So… What do you think?" He seemed impatient waiting on an answer.

I glanced up at him then stared back down at the magical-looking cottage. "It's wonderful."

Jonathan finished what was left in his glass, placing it back to the table. A happy impression overcame his tired face, and he casually rubbed his hands in enjoyment. "Grand." He spoke with eagerness. "That's just grand."

Why so grand? I thought to myself. Only to be beaten abruptly by the answer.

"I'm giving it to you. It's all yours, Les."

I half expected my brother to be pulling my chain, or even some kind of catch to be involved, but there was not. He stood looking into my eyes, not an ounce of humour displayed on his face. I was in utter disbelief. A thousand questions swam through my mind, but only one of any real importance to me.

"Why would you do this for me?"

It didn't take him a moment to provide me with an explanation.

"Well… You deserve it, Les. It wasn't fair for the rest of us to leave you the way we did. It's probably the reason you never got a break in life." He paused for a second. "This is your chance, Les." Now it sounded more like he was trying to persuade me than an offer. "This is your chance to leave it all behind, start over. And not just a new home, a new place, new people, a new life."

Taking in each and every word Jonathan spoke, I placed the piece of paper down that had my full attention for the past few minutes. I didn't say another word to him, nor him to me. But I held out my hand in order to shake his. A grin appeared on my brother's pale face. He graciously obliged the offer by shaking my hand heartily. More papers now appeared from his pocket and into my view.

"This is the full address of the house. Also, here's the sales agent's number that will meet you at the property. I don't hold the keys, you see. But it's important you leave tomorrow. I will get in contact with the agent to meet you there."

I smiled, only too happy to agree with his terms. This time without any hesitation.

Before I left the room to get another beverage, one question did come to mind, and now seemed as good a time as any to ask.

"John, how did you get into the house? I swear I locked the door before leaving."

A slight smirk flew over my brother's face once more, as if some dazzling trick had been performed that evening. However, the magic was soon broken. He explained he had surprisingly stumbled on a set of house keys, lying only a foot away from the door. The keys themselves were left abandoned in a puddle of rainwater.

Back into the living area, Jonathan stood to accept his drink. I soon realised the man seemed more out of sorts than he was previously. His skin tone also began to grow paler by the second. With his glass in hand, he fell backwards into the chair and harshly rubbed at his temples with both hands.

"I'm sorry about this." Jonathan's face was slightly hidden by the palms of his large hands.

"I haven't been feeling great on the journey back here, Les. I'm sure I blacked out for a little while. Must be all the stress, I guess. I just need a good rest."

It didn't feel like it was my place to question his emotional state. After all, he hadn't been a part of my life for many years. Upon finishing his second glass of whisky, I told him to get some rest. He indeed looked like he needed it. And to be completely truthful, so did I.

I was about to leave him there, lying on the sofa, when his whispered voice called back to me.

"It's good to see you again, Les." Both his eyes remained tightly shut as he lay comfortably curled to his side.

I decided not to reply but left him to rest. Quietly, I withdrew from the room, leaving him with only the dim light of a corner lamp to keep Jonathan familiar with the long-forgotten surroundings.

Chapter Five

The sound of the alarm sharply drilled into my ears, unpleasantly waking me from what seemed to be the best night's sleep I'd had in some time. Peace and quiet now fell through the house. My forehead slowly sank back into the covers. It wasn't long before the memories of the previous evening came flooding back to mind.

Hesitating for some time on whether to get up and make my way downstairs, I slowly crept along the landing, attempting not to disturb my fatigued guest who slumbered peacefully below. The living room door remained tightly shut. Once I reached the lower floor of the house, I diverted straight into the kitchen. Not forgetting I had company, I began to prepare our beverages.

With my hand resting against the living room door, I paused, then decided to knock before entering.

"Jonathan?"

There was no response. The man must have been more exhausted than I'd expected.

Walking straight into the darkened room without a care, I whispered again. "I didn't want to wake you," I said, only this time in a slightly louder tone.

There was no daylight, the blackout curtains had seen to that. *No wonder he hasn't awoken*. I placed the mugs down as I looked over towards the sofa. The bundle of ruffled blankets that had hidden Jonathan peacefully beneath, remained unmoved.

"Rain's on its way again" I said observing the quiet street with a twitch of the curtain.

Witnessing the gloomy street, I happened to recall a memory of Jonathan that had me chuckling. A memory surfaced I thought had long since been forgotten. He had just turned twenty and, like any other young man, Jonathan had a talent for sneaking ladies back into the house after dark. It was a practise that was highly frowned upon by our parents, though it caused no fear in the heart of Jonathan. And if my memory serves me correctly, he had got pretty good at it, too. That was until our mother waited up one night. When she found out, she gave him a battering in front of the entire family, including the girl he had smuggled into the house, who just sat still with shock.

Running from the house, Mother chased him down the street with a floor brush in hand, vigorously swiping, missing his head by an inch. Funny thing is, he never tried it again after that. "Jonathan, do you remember…"

I took a sip of my beverage and somehow burnt my upper lip in the process, cursing as the mug fell to the floor. Its entire contents spread wildly across the faded carpet, but the commotion did not disturb Jonathan, nor did his hidden body move in reaction.

I looked at the clusters of covers with slight concern and quickly unfolded a section, knowing well enough where his head lay at rest. Although now, nothing was there. With the covers stripped instantly, all that remained beneath was a grooved shape of where he had previously slept.

Jonathan was no longer there.

Standing in disbelief, I desperately searched the rooms in order to find him, but it was no good. The man had not just slipped from sight, he was gone.

He must have left in the early hours of the morning. And as quietly as he arrived.

It was the only explanation. I sat and pondered my thoughts further, wondering if my dear brother's appearance was nothing but a dream. Or worse. An unwanted medication effect from Dr Carson's pills.

A full glass of whisky stood untouched upon a coaster, and several items on the table remained sturdily in place. These items were, however, familiar to me. I picked up the pieces of paper that displayed the old stone cottage, again scanning its text.

"Leave today, that's what he said," I muttered. Like a child receiving gifts aplenty on Christmas morning, a smile was now permanently fixed. My watch displayed seven twenty a.m. "There's definitely still time."

I quickly ran up the stairs in order to pack for my anticipated departure.

Echoes of Home

Chapter Six

P acking certainly wasn't difficult. Neither was saying goodbye. After all, there was no one to tell. No one to hold me back, pleading desperately for my stay. Though, I suppose it was all for the best. I despised farewells and having to tolerate the pressured guilt of someone inclining you to stay.

I was finally placing this rotten past behind. With the house left empty, I decided it was best to pass the keys, including a short letter, round to the neighbour at number ten, an elderly lady my mother had thought of fondly throughout her life. And a lady whom I knew I could trust.

My fingers trembled as I knotted them tightly around the cases and allowed the front door to slam promptly behind me. Placing the last of the luggage into the tiny car was somewhat challenging, though. I'd never packed for such an occasion.

Soon I was finally ready to leave. The strange thing was, I couldn't recall looking back at my childhood home that morning. Without hesitation or regret, I placed the key into the ignition and keenly drove from the kerb and out of view of the street.

The same old town flew by without notice. I never considered if there would come a time when I would glare upon these sorrowful streets again.

No matter. I thought. I couldn't say they'd be missed. The very idea of returning to Stoke left a deep rooted and unpleasant grasp within my gut. No, there would be no homecoming. There'd be no need for one. And I would do everything within my ability to make it so.

If only things had turned out better. Not everything of course. I had long since grown accustomed to the fact that nothing in life was handed freely. Although, it was evident, some didn't fight quite as hard to reach their wildest ambitions. I think because of this, I just stopped trying. What was the point after all? In any of it? The very incentive to lose your life, breaking your back working, all for the sake of a miserable promotion. That's not forgetting the unnoticeable forty pence hourly increase that came in hand. It just didn't seem worth the bother. And with that state of mind, I let go of it all. Education, work progression, hobbies. It all went down the toilet. And then there was Kate.

Ah, yes, sweet darling Kate. We struck paths in high school, although we acknowledged each other several years prior to dating. She was a catch. A real heart throb at that. Though, things were different back then. I was different back then. The childish relationship of high school dwindled into an almost adult relationship, and far too rapidly for anyone's liking. We did everything together, *I mean everything.* I didn't care. I liked her. I mean, *really, really* liked her. And it wasn't until she was gone, I'd come to realise the love I never gave. She was funny, clever, a real smart case, with a future prospect in medicine. I looked back at her humour fondly, almost as much as her looks. She was a pretty sort. Everyone thought so, with an overpowering attitude to better herself as well as the people she stuck to. That's where it all fell apart for us. As soon as she passed that driving test. As soon as those delicate hands firmly gripped the leather of a steering wheel, her foot fell flat to the pedal. She wanted gone. Stoke just wasn't enough anymore. Or maybe I just wasn't enough. I couldn't just leave, either. I had responsibilities and commitments. I didn't see it then. Her ideas seemed nothing more than rash and careless. If only after all these years, I could tell her truly how I felt back then. Instead, I allowed her to slip through my fingers and venture on without me. We spoke on the kerb one evening, our decision to split seeming almost mutual. Kate cried, I didn't. She was being idiotic. Acting childishly towards a notion that in time would see her the fool. Still, I couldn't help but feel some form of guilt. Tears fell from her glazed eyes, falling to the soft blonde curl that fell freely from her shoulders. And just like that, it was over. My first and last love over. *Last love so far,* I thought while passing Kate's former home.

It was surprising to hear, Kate shamefully returned to Stoke some years later, though we never made contact again. Arriving back home with five children may have had something to do with it. One of which, only a babe in arms. She'd certainly been busy. And married too, apparently. Settled down with a window cleaner who ironically adopted the name of Dick. I'd see her around from time to time. Though unfortunately, our eyes never met. And our paths never crossed. However, none of that mattered now. It was a lifetime ago. A childish love story that ran its limited course. But still, first love memories never really fade.

Entering onto the motorway with a heavy foot, I had a nine-hour drive ahead of me and was willing to make the journey in good time. With the radio blasting and the road ahead long, I knew my circumstances would lead me to a new adventure. That, in turn, made me feel the happiest I'd felt in a long, long time. I'd forgotten to plan the trip accurately, so I rummaged through my inner coat pockets, attempting to find the pieces of paper that held the full address of the house. With no such luck, I pulled over in order to properly map my route. At first, entering the direction address into the navigation system appeared impossible, although, casting my mind back, Jonathan had stated the house sat in an isolated spot. So, giving up on the idea of setting the coordinates to the exact location, I did the next best thing, setting it to the closest village to where the house stood.

I was making surprisingly good time and even managing to take a couple of short stops along the way, checking my watch continuously as my hand drummed on the steering wheel. My only pressing worry was that I wouldn't get there before nightfall, although the thought didn't put me off at all. I had been sufficiently ensured that the sales agent would meet me personally to hand over the keys, plus any other important documentation I might require.

I reached Glasgow around three. The built-up area reminded me so much of the town I had just left hours prior. The busy lifestyle seemed to interest me no longer, and the more I thought about it, the more I longed for peace. I'd thought of it often while working or pushing my way through the busy towns, each and every person desperately shoving the next, blinded by their own snotty self-importance. Yes, the quiet life sounded so much more appealing to me now. And that was exactly what I was going to get.

The farther I drove, the more country lands appeared and the dramatic wastelands vastly spread open into view. At some points you could see for miles, or so it seemed. It really made one wonder how the hell anything really survived out here. The northern roads for miles proved uneventful. Busy roads meant no scenery, and by the time I finally reached Inverness, the sun had already begun to set, and the darker it got, the more challenging the Highland roads ahead of me became.

After I crossed Kessock Bridge, the road steadily took me towards the small boating town of Ullapool. From here, only a short distance lay between me and my soon-to-be new home.

"Christ, I gotta take a piss," I mumbled over the loud radio tunes, half glaring at the now-empty water bottle that continually rocked from side to side on the passenger seat. As luck would have it, a tourist sign suddenly swung into view. It crookedly stuck out from the grass verge, slowly over time, peeking out onto the roadside. It read *Knockan Crag Public facilities*.

Perfect timing.

I made the sharp right turning off the road, desperately wanting to relieve myself from the pressing discomfort. I stepped out onto the dusty car park, and the radio faded to silence in the background as I walked.

An old tourist map hung crudely against the wall of the building. It clearly displayed my location, and although the image itself was faded due to the time of day, it also presented the two small lochs that sat just across from where I stood. The first, Loch An Ais, and slightly beyond that was Loch Fada. On return from the restroom, I paused, leaning casually on the fully opened door of the car, taking a brief moment to stare at the peaceful view before me. The lochs gleamed in harmony as they caught the reflection of the evening sky.

Echoes of Home

Chapter Seven

The destination point was quickly approaching. Concentrating intently, I was now down to only a single lane with limited passing points. And although I gazed with impatience, it was now almost impossible to notice any kind of landmark indicating I was where I needed to be.

Hitting the brakes, I slowed right down after noticing a hanging sign to my left. It read *Elphin Café*. The café itself looked almost derelict in the twilight, but more importantly, I was on the right track.

With no indication of life inside the café, all I could do was continue to drive. Thankfully no cars had driven in sight for some miles, so I decreased my speed through the isolated village. It seemed like the best approach, and of course, caused no potential hazard to locals nearby.

My route sent me drifting out of the sleepy village and along a narrow Highland lane. Tall grass had protruded in clumps through the road's centre, and at either side, bushes stood tall in thickness, enclosing the road's entry farther ahead. That was when I saw it. Completely cut off from the world, a large gate swung into view. A Property For Sale notice desperately struggled to remain attached to its bars, flapping wildly in the breeze. The sign itself had been visibly damaged by the elements, now showing only a faded outline of lettering that once, I'm sure, displayed boldly. I believed this was, in fact, the place I was searching for.

"Yup... This is it." I exhaled with a sigh of relief as the turning headlights shone out onto the lonesome path ahead.

Driving past the iron gates led me down a long, enclosed driveway, the passage taking me completely from sight of the road. The car's main beam threw a cold, shadowy light over the unoccupied land around me, and once I passed the overgrown hedges and crumbling walls of the entrance, the view of the cottage crept into view. The place I was to now call home.

My vehicle was brought to a permanent stop for the first time in four hundred and ninety miles and was now left to peacefully slumber for the remainder of the night. My back sharply stiffened with pain when I moved sluggishly from the long-seated position.

I looked up to the night sky and then down to the shadowed house, momentarily stretching to loosen the discomfort that sat unpleasantly between my joints. I circled my stance, and a frown settled swiftly across my puzzled face, the conclusion quickly hitting me that no one was here to meet me. Not a soul.

I swiftly peered through the small black windows of the cottage in the hope someone waited for my arrival. It was doubtful. It seemed rather evident that no message had been left by the sales agent my brother had mentioned to me. No, there was nothing. No sales agent, no message. And no indication in sight that anyone had even been here prior to my arrival. Frustrated was not a strong enough description of my emotions at that moment. To have no one meet me here was absolutely unbelievable, and damn well unprofessional, considering the lengthy journey that I'd made that day.

Back at the car, I collected my phone and pulled the papers ruthlessly from my inner pocket. I punched the numbers in a desperate attempt to call the sales agent and give him a piece of my mind. The signal dropped immediately upon call.

Another kick in the teeth, is it?

Furious, with no other plan of action, I strained to look for houses nearby, desperately hoping maybe, just maybe, someone would kindly allow me to use their telephone. Though I soon had to face facts. There was not a house light in sight. I thought back on my journey. The last building I recalled was the café some five miles back, but that would most certainly be of no help in my current situation.

The wind fiercely brewed, throwing gravel across the ground that once lay firmly settled. I clenched at the collar of my coat, instantly accepting the open space made the weather appear far worse than it evidently was.

Kicking the ground in raging anger, I cursed words I felt not at all appropriate to repeat. Determination had indeed turned into despair. As my back fell harshly against the wall of the cottage to rest, my arm effortlessly swung down, my palm rebounding from the stone and my phone slipping from grasp. I recovered the device that now lay hidden amongst the uncut grass, and the slight sound of chimes caught my attention. I had to glance twice before noticing, but to my disbelief, a set of rattling keys gently swayed from the rear door of the cottage.

"I don't believe…" Rather than finishing my sentence, I instead kept quiet, walking steadily towards the rear door of the house.

Half expecting someone to stumble out from where I roamed, I took hold of the keys that still solidly rested in the keyhole and unlocked the door. The handle was stiff and rusted into place. With plenty of effort, it soon gave way and with a jolt of strength, the door released from its firm hold.

I peered through the narrow crack, my face pinned tightly against its rotting frame. The room inside appeared empty at first. With no light source in sight, the inner room remained dark and a mystery to any guest. Opening the door fully proved nothing more than a struggle. Vast overgrowth had made its way up onto the doorstep, creating weed-tangling knots as it caught and climbed onto any object made available in its path. Still, with a bit of force, pushing myself through the small gap seemed light work, and despite my uneasiness, I willingly continued forward. My bodily shape disappearing from sight.

Chapter Eight

I must've dozed off, awaking in a panicked state, completely forgetting my whereabouts. It took me a moment to gain my bearings of the room in which I lay. The grandfather clock behind me struck the hour, and I suddenly woke from my sound sleep. As I scrambled from my position, it was visible that the towered clock had struck two a.m. My watch somehow displayed differently, indicating the time of ten p.m.

"Bloody battery's dead," I said, repeatedly tapping the watch's face, allowing myself to scramble back into place.

It was more than noticeable that the roaring fire that had once been was now nothing but glowing embers. Forcefully closing both eyes to once again fall victim of sleep, I couldn't help but feel a cold draft that circulated the room continuously. Groaning, I attempted to ignore the unpleasant chill by curling further into the softness of the cushions.

The cold did not subside. I managed to pull myself up from the ever-so-comfy position and again slumped to my knees in order to revive the pleasurable warmth of the fire. With difficulty, I forced my eyes to remain open.

I placed several logs on the grate, quickly reaching for the small box of matches. It took several attempts to strike the head of the first match, which was then thrown onto the fire, followed in turn by the second and third.

It was at that point something odd grabbed my attention. It was a sound, not by any means a natural noise. No, this was a tapping. A tapping on glass. Going by first impressions, my immediate guess was that of a tree branch gently swaying, hitting the living room window. As I recalled, the wind had indeed been strong that evening, but it wasn't long before that idea was soon dismissed. The sound itself had too much of a regularity to its pattern. This was not a noise of an object hitting the window with each gust of wind. The thought sent a shiver up my spine. This was a gentle knock, almost as if someone was trying to innocently gain attention from outside.

The tapping continued. Not bluntly or aggressively, but persistent nonetheless. The echoing and haunting sound bounced from wall to wall, determined to be heard.

Desperately seeking an explanation for such an unusual sound, I certainly wouldn't be able to find one on my knees in front of the fireplace.

The sales agent maybe? Again, I quickly dismissed the idea, due to the time the old clock indicated.

Standing to my feet, my mind now fixed on the only place where the tapping noise would emanate. I staggered slowly towards the window, gazing suspiciously at the outside world, making out only the hazed images of my car, parked directly in front of the cottage and an unoccupied wooden bench that sat directly below the windowsill. Any other external view appeared to be partially blocked by my own strong reflection.

Still, the effortless tapping went on. I continued to peer out through the glass, tunnelling my vision in the process. My own mirrored image stalled my judgment. Swiftly turning to place the room in complete darkness, I suddenly froze. A cold sweat fell from my brow, accompanied by a large lump that remained lodged within the very centre of my throat. The door leading into the corridor was now wide open. The same door that I distinctly remembered closing upon my arrival.

Beyond the entrance of the living room now became a fearful mystery to me. What was to my knowledge an empty cottage, now seemed empty no longer. The thought that someone could have entered and watched me sleep soundly that evening disturbed me some. And although jumping to a conclusion, I couldn't help think it.

I stood as if called to attention, fear and confusion clouding my brain. Still, not a soul stood in place along the isolated hallway.

I remained stationary for a few seconds more, focusing one hundred percent of my attention to the darkness beyond the room. Staring intently, I waited for any movement to occur that would prove my theory correct.

The fire crackled and whistled as air abruptly escaped from the burning wood, heightening my senses in the process, snapping me from the hypnotic trace that had imprisoned me. I wanted answers, *but to what risk*? After all, I hadn't investigated the rest of the cottage that evening. It could have easily been possible that someone was already upstairs. Or worse, in the locked room across the hall from where I stood.

Slowly, I crept across the living room, again each step more noticeable than the last. The tapping sound continued to torment me, its pattern now appearing to quicken in speed. Beads of sweat rolled from my forehead. My heartbeat drummed through my ears at the sudden thought of greeting the cause of this haunting sound. My breathing suddenly quickened. The sensation of pins and needles rapidly pulsated through all my fingers, leaving my upper arms with a strong sense of numbness.

I shook my head. "You're letting the darkness get the better of you." I spoke the words quietly, my eyes tightly closed, slowing my breathing in order to calm my nerves.

I decided enough was enough and gave myself a short countdown from three, readying myself to prepare for the worst. My legs trembled as I stepped out into the darkness of the corridor. Yet no one was present. And now, there was only silence that filled the house.

Echoes of Home

Chapter Nine

It goes without saying that the first night's sleep hadn't been the greatest. A bright beam of morning light shone through the small window and directly on where I lay, betraying thousands of dust specks that floated peacefully around its air space.

My eyes again remained firmly shut, and I manoeuvred my position out of the sun's beam. The mobile phone that was tucked away inside my jeans pocket had slid from its place and now rested screen side down on the floor, covered in ash from the fire that had long since died.

The time was nine-fifteen a.m.

The day has not been wasted.

Not allowing myself to drift off back to sleep, I sat up to escape the tiring daze that bogged my mind. Last night had certainly been a strange turn of events, but now it seemed like nothing more than an unpleasant dream, blocking out the feeling of fear and insecurity. The rest of the night had proven completely uneventful. However, sleep became troublesome, as I still waited intently for the next unwelcoming sound to occur.

Already dressed, I inspected the somewhat large, outdated kitchen, raiding the cupboards and shelves in the hope that some form of stored food would be available to me. It was hopeless. The kitchen supplied nothing more than dust sheets on every shelf, as well as shattered wall tiles that lay strewn across its damaged wooden floor, leaving me with no other alternative than to lace up my boots.

I prepared to make my way to the closest general store. Although it was sunny, a sharp, cooling breeze hit against my back, pushing me forward as I stepped on to the path. The landscape appeared far clearer now. My surroundings were stunning, beautiful, in fact. Vast valleys that had been touched only by nature, rippling brooks that fed into a giant loch. On either side of this loch stood two marvellous mountains, dominating the area in the distance, clustered with small woodlands scattered alongside their bases.

To my recollection, the paper that Jonathan handed me a few days prior named these two mountains Sullivan and Cull Mhor?… Cull Moor? I couldn't quite remember. However, I was unable to identify them by name regardless.

It truly was a fantastic setting, and as I scanned the scenery around me, it took only a moment to realise this cottage was the only settlement in view at all. Coming to terms with how isolated I'd be, and how vast the rural landscape was, didn't come easy. I couldn't help but think, if it wasn't for my vehicle, I would be completely screwed. The nearest lodging was the café that sat some miles away, which in the case of an emergency would take hours to reach by foot in such rough terrain.

That's not helping.

I shook the negative thoughts aside.

Inside the car was just as bitter, and turning on the heater, although blowing only cold air, was a natural instinct. The car was put into reverse and slowly began to creep back down the steep, unlevel driveway.

For a split second, I focused on something and brought the car to a sudden halt. Adjusting my rear-view mirror to get a clearer image, I soon unbuckled my seatbelt, eagerly stepping out of the car for a more promising view. Due to the harsh morning breeze, it was difficult to focus on my target, but on the other side of the valley, on a hill near the very edge of the brook, stood another stone cottage. It was impossible to tell if it was occupied due to my distance, but nevertheless, I found the image surprisingly uplifting. To know there were others settled within the same lands as myself gave me some peace of mind. And, of course, when the opportunity would first present itself, I would take the time and make a proper introduction to the new so-called neighbours.

Back in the car, I looked once more into the rear-view mirror. The image of the cottage was now so much clearer and magnified compared to my previous observation. It was so much easier to make out the dark-grey stone of the cottage walls. My concentration was broken by the rumbling of my stomach that sat desperately awaiting fuel.

And on that note, it was only a moment before I was driving back on the main Highland road, only too happy to take in the brilliant scenery that surrounded me. And for a brief moment I forgot all about the stone cottage that sat across the valley from my own.

Chapter Ten

In daylight, the small café situated at Elphin village appeared much more inviting. I luckily arrived just as the sign was turned from closed to open.

I sat at one of the few wooden tables. The waitress took my order right away and wasn't shying back. I ordered a large cooked breakfast with extra bacon and eggs, a side of toast, a glass of orange juice, and a pot of coffee to get me ready for the day ahead.

The waitress seemed pleasant enough and took it upon her own curiosity to ask if I was passing through the area. Just as I began to reply to the lady's somewhat pleasant face, she was called away by a female member of staff who looked unappealingly scruffy compared to her work colleague. Nevertheless, the waitress left my table, offering her apologies for the disruption.

I looked around the café with interest. On the right side of the dining area stood a general supply corner. It was filled with your basic essential items such as bread, milk, eggs, tinned food, toiletries, et cetera. With not driving past another store *en route*, this would be a lifesaver for today and possibly for the days to come.

My pot of coffee arrived at the table with a smile from the waitress. I spent the next few minutes without a care in the world, reading the local newspaper, effortlessly humming to recognisable tunes that came out through the café's distorted radio.

As soon as the breakfast arrived, I didn't hesitate in tucking in. It was delicious.

My compliments to the scruffy chef.

I smiled to myself, trying my best to hold back an awkward snigger, while discreetly licking my greasy fingers. This breakfast was indeed the first proper cooked meal I'd had in some time and without a doubt gave me a feeling of comfort as I rested back against the chair.

As I lifted the glass of juice to my lips, the café door swung open aggressively, slamming and rebounding against the interior wall, almost shattering the glass pane. A gentleman walked in, wedging the door fully open behind him. The fact that the man was clearly from around these parts quickly became apparent. He greeted both of the café employees on a first-name basis, along with a friendly wave. At first glance I would say the gentleman looked to be a farmer, and to that point, a farmer who had lived a hard life.

As he spoke to the girls behind the counter, completely unaware of my presence, I eyed the rough-looking figure up and down inquisitively.

Late sixties maybe, early seventies at my best guess.

A grey flat cap, stained with paint markings, rested on his head. This revealed long, uncut white hair that curled into the inner collar of his shirt. He had on a brown jacket, black combats, and green Wellington boots that had covered the café floor in thick mud prints from the entrance to serving hatch.

"Yup… Definitely a farmer." I spoke much louder than intended.

It was unfortunate, but at that moment, the gentleman spotted me and regained his upright posture at the counter. Without hesitation or boundaries, the man walked straight over, expressionless. Pulling out a chair, allowing the feet to screech across the tiled floor, he rested only two tables away from where I sat.

Awkwardness didn't even cut it. This man willingly continued to stare me out while I so immaturely pretended to gander through the café newspaper, in the hope of avoiding his inquisitive glare.

"Two month old," the elderly man grumbled in a somewhat louder tone than expected.

Startled at the sudden outburst, "Excuse me?" I asked, my eyes now in direct contact with the man opposite me.

To my confusion, he sat sternly shaking his head as if a father disappointed by his son's failures. He then swiftly nodded in the direction of where his comment was intended.

"The paper, laddie, the paper, it's near on two months old." His Scottish accent was far too broad for my liking or understanding.

A slight smirk appeared on his face. He was indeed correct. Folding up the outdated paper, I now had no choice but to indulge this local man with further conversation.

"Thank you, I would never have noticed." I slurped at the remainder of my beverage, wishfully thinking this would bring an end to the already awkward conversation.

"Ah, sure you would've. The name's Coull. Might I enquire as to yours?"

He paused for a brief moment, the smirk now vanished as I tried to interpret the strong northern accent into more familiar understanding.

He continued. "Nae sure I've seen you around here before, lad. Just passin' through?"

He spoke in a somewhat gravelled tone, making it only too obvious he had smoked for many years, struggling to finish each of his questions without bringing a pale-blue handkerchief to his mouth. He infectiously coughed aloud in my direction. His questioning seemed instant, and due to the manner in which he asked, I could see he was a man who demanded a straight answer.

His coughing annoyingly persisted, and regardless of whether he could hear me or not, I decided to reply.

"Leslie Wills, from Staffordshire, and no, not passing through."

Just about finishing his coughing fit, he looked up at me puzzled, tucking his handkerchief away in the chest pocket of his shirt. His facial expression remained confused, but no more confused than the face that stared back at him. His line of sight finally altered from my own as he bent his head, giving the back of his dirt-covered neck a good, long scratch.

"Well, I know all these parts, laddie. And there's no' any free lodgings nearby for miles. Where might ye be staying at exactly?"

Again, the old man waited silently for an answer. It was an answer I was not happy in sharing at this particular time. However, I entertained him with the reply he desperately needed.

"Elphin Cottage." I said, wondering if I'd even pronounced its title correctly.

The old man's expression abruptly changed as the lines on his forehead deepened, and he continued to nod, staring at the mud-printed trail he had proudly made on the floor.

"A dark past," he gravely muttered, lifting his eyebrows highly, only to nod in agreement with his own curious statement.

I wasn't indulging him in the matter, neither did I want to question his enigmatically strange remark. I took another sip of my coffee and gently pushed the now finished plates to the side of the table.

The elderly man had risen to his feet, tipped his hat in a gentleman-like fashion, and casually walked out into the blustery morning.

What the hell was that about?

The thought raced through my mind. Observing the man as he struggled to make the first climb up into his truck, I pondered on the reaction of his nervousness.

Something definitely wasn't right with his response, and to be truthful, his statement had put me slightly on edge. It was now or never to find out what he'd truly meant by his remark.

I rushed to the door in the desperate hope to catch him before he departed. I quickly made a small gesture to the waitress that I would be but a brief moment. She smiled and nodded, and I pushed aggressively on the door that clearly displayed Pull.

The wind was still as strong as when I first ventured out that morning. By the time I reached the vehicle that Mr Coull had entered, I pleaded to myself that some form of rational explanation would be given to his unwelcoming comment.

"Mr Coull?" I yelled through the dirt-layered glass.

At first, no acknowledgement was given. It was almost as if he expected me to be present at his side. Rolling down his window, sighing loud enough for me to hear, he looked at me as though the conversation we'd only just shared, in fact didn't take place.

"It's not Mr Coull, lad, it's just Coull," he stated in an impatient manner. Again, he pulled the handkerchief from his pocket, without doubt to burst into another coughing fit.

"I'm sorry, sir, what did you mean by that?" I projected my voice in order to be heard over the howling wind and rattling truck engine.

"What?" he replied promptly, gasping for air as his infernal coughing continued.

I was frustrated. My body tensed in reaction, for me to only repeat the exact same question. Again, I explained myself further.

"Just then, in the café, sir, you said, 'A dark past'. What's wrong with the cottage?"

He sighed once more, placing his mucus-filled handkerchief back into his pocket. He looked past his windscreen and onto the distant lands. His jaw hung open slightly, attempting to provide me with answers that were not so easy to give.

"Look, laddie, it's no' Elphin Cottage. It's… Well… it's what it sits across from. Locals are suspicious enough round these parts. They won't go near the place if it can be helped. Do yourself a favour, lad, don't wander the lands. Keep to the house when the skies are at their greyest. It will prevent you questioning and hassling folk."

Hesitating with my reply, I thought for a second, then decided to respond rationally.

"But… There's nothing out there but wilderness, sir. Nothing for miles for that matter." I shrugged in confused protest.

Both his hands remained firmly gripped on the steering wheel. However, his dazed line of sight altered from the far distance and now to where I stood. "Then you hav'nae spotted it yet, have you, lad?"

I remained speechless as I watched the man who spoke to me in riddles.

"Good for you, lad. Many a year folks see things they dare not speak of. Hell, I've seen things from time to time myself, and without doubt, lad, so will you."

His remark was not one to frighten me, his manner remained calm and casual. All I could do was ponder his words. I was given no time to indulge him further on the subject. His truck jerked forward, my hand sliding along the surface of the moving vehicle's paintwork. Off the café premises the truck rolled, and soon, into the distance, producing nothing but a cloudy dust trail that filled the air behind it, appearing like a darkened mist.

Chapter Eleven

I considered what he said, watching the truck fade slowly from sight. But still, there was no answer in the man's unexplained ramblings. This, however, wouldn't stop me from questioning myself further.

I stumbled back inside the café, the dust still settling as it floated through the air behind me. How could just a few words have completely turned my day around? And just when this simple village café started to feel homely.

I asked the pleasant waitress for the bill, and she happily obliged.

"Anything else sir?" she asked. The same cheerful smile appeared gracefully, displaying bold dimples on both cheeks. Not forgetting the general supplies before I left, I grabbed what was needed and departed from the café.

Outside, a tall notice board rattled loosely from the slats of a side wall. The notices attached, well protected by a thick plastic panel held firmly in place to the frame. I stepped over, juggling the supplies that seemed to drop from underarm. The advertisements were few and far between. The majority were faded, having been exposed to countless days of light. Still, I panned through the jumble of cards regardless.

On the board, there were tour days, fishing trips, Boat hires, an address for a local B&B, and an unreadable card posted back from three years prior. I was about to give up, when the final notice caught my eye. It read; *Help wanted. For seasonal work only. Contact Michael.* To be truthful, I hadn't considered the idea of work. My only ambition was to get here fast. I had money. But it would only see me through to the summer months at best. No, I needed a job. And if my plan was to stay put, I'd have to find one quickly. I just needed time to settle.

Flinging the supplies onto the passenger seat, my mind casually wandered. I hadn't any plans for the remainder of the day, and it was still early. Although I wanted nothing more than to locate a rustic Scottish bar, the best idea was probably to return back to Elphin Cottage and unpack the belongings that still sat cluttered in the car. There was also the matter of taking a good look around the remainder of the cottage, something that completely slipped my mind since venturing out that morning.

Thinking nothing more of the subject, I returned through the sharp twisting lanes of the Highland valleys until, once again, I was back to my somewhat familiar territory of neglected roads.

I climbed out of the car. The sun shone down on where I stood, casting a completely different appearance on the cottage and grounds surrounding me. The bright colour of the wild flowers that sprang along the grounds of the house, combined with the rich greenery that filled the lands in the distance, really brought the place to life.

The weeds around the foot of the rear door again proved a nuisance as I struggled to squeeze through the confined gap, hoping not to drop a single item. The kitchen, of course, remained exactly as I'd left it that very morning. The light shone brightly on the worktops, revealing layers of grime and filth that had been left undisturbed for years.

A few cleaning products were already available to me from under the ceramic sink. The job of tidying seemed to last forever. When finished, both arms were left with a dull ache that stiffened my shoulders.

Thank God for that, I thought breathlessly.

I rested for a second against the counter, admiring my work. Complaining aside, the job was done, and although only a small task, it was a large tick off my to-do list.

I collected the rest of my homely possessions from the car. The weather remained pleasant and got the better of me. The wooden bench that rested just beneath the windowsill looked too inviting to dismiss.

Sitting only a moment, I lapped up the sun's rays for as long as possible before a small cluster of clouds briefly blocked the glare and warmth of the sun. My sight now displayed a bleached vision. The flowers and fields that had stood so lively with colour, now stood colourless. But I knew in time my vision would return to normal and the beautiful hues that surrounded me would soon drain back into sight.

Gripping my knees to support my upper body, I stretched and resumed the job at hand. I transferred each bag from the boot of my car in an orderly fashion, locking it for the final time that day. Prior to hastily organising the gathered baggage, a sudden shrieking screeched from above me.

Glancing to the sky, I gasped with astonishment. It was an eagle. What kind of eagle I couldn't be sure, but it effortlessly circled me, twitching its head, while scouting for prey far below.

The luggage can wait.

I marvelled at the sight of this beautiful creature as it paraded the sky above me.

This intimidating bird continued to glide proudly for some time, then broke its circular scouting pattern, flying into the distant view.

The wonderment of nature truly was astonishing, which, in turn, had me feeling much gratitude as I stood observing its beauty that day. I watched as the bird flew farther and farther away, the camouflage of the mountains soon to take over the bird's very existence.

I was gratified by the marvellous creature that was now no longer visible. My gaze now skittered over to the old cottage that sat across the moor from my own. It was then I saw it.

Echoes of Home

Chapter Twelve

I wasn't sure who, or even what it was I saw that day, but standing at the edge of the brook, down the hill from the unknown cottage itself, stood a figure. A figure almost hidden by the shadows of its surrounding landscape. Its tilted face appeared sickly white, and its body appeared rake-like with starvation. It glared only in my direction, its sunken eyes gazing on where I stood.

Was this nothing more than a trick of the light? I continued to observe, and it became clear the figure was not about to reveal itself as an illusion. So still – ever so still – as if almost inhuman. It didn't move, did not budge. Not even the cooling breeze affected movement of its dark, withered clothing that hung loosely from its skeleton-like frame.

Holding up my hand in an attempt to make a waving gesture, caused further unpleasantness. There was no change of expression from the figure in return. It glared only at me, or through me.

"Who are you?" I muttered.

Only the breeze replied with a distant howl. Yet, the figure remained motionless. In one hand it held some kind of object that I struggled to identify at first glance.

A bucket or lantern maybe?

With both hands cupped towards my face, I shouted, slowly edging down the path. My sight stayed fixated on the sad soul staring back at me.

With each step, the facial features stood out more clearly.

Stumbling on what appeared to be a small gully in the cobbled path, I landed face-first, my head rebounding harshly from the wet stone causing me to lose grip of my phone in the process. I took no interest in my injury, instantly regaining my feet. I quickly dusted the dirt from my sleeves, eager to once again gain sight of the distant figure.

I looked again, and again, but the figure was now gone. I continued to survey the area where it had appeared, though it was no good. The figure had vanished along with the nice weather. Grey clouds dominated the sky from the south, painting a dullness over the lands that seconds ago were wild with life.

The pain from my fall heightened as I limped pathetically back to the gathered luggage. I made multiple trips to the car, each time repeatedly checking the distant area. The land was isolated. However, the feeling of being watched lingered.

Back inside, and slightly shaken, I made sure the door was securely bolted behind me. Instead of taking the cases upstairs immediately, I first took a quick look around to see if one of the rooms was more to my liking. Both were in fact identical in size, providing a single bed as well as the usual bedroom furniture. The only obvious difference was that the first room had a front-facing window and the second a rear.

I decided it best to take the front-facing bedroom. It offered me a view of unannounced callers and the road that led to the cottage itself.

I collapsed on the hard mattress. I felt the blood pulsating through my arms, my heartbeat pounding heavily in my ears. I lifted my knee into view, as if to perform some kind of yoga exercise. It revealed jagged scuffs through my trousers, and underneath that, an unsightly swollen kneecap. "Ah, great." I spoke with annoyance, letting my leg fall back onto the mattress.

Inhaling deeply, I had the biggest intention not to stay resting on the bed, but somehow my forearm managed to place itself over my eyes in order to block out the daylight.

Chapter Thirteen

Of course, I fell asleep. Rubbing my eyes to persuade myself to stay awake, I checked my watch, knowing all too well it would still display the time of ten pm. The old bedsheet was wrapped around me tightly as I sat up.

The wind sounded much stronger than earlier. With each gust, it felt as though the cottage ever so slightly shook from the ground up. The clouds were now a darkened grey, which would most probably mean continuous rain throughout the evening. This would, without doubt, bring more unwanted surprises to the cottage.

I peered through the small bedroom window. The cottage in the distance remained in view although blurred in appearance, as condensation lay smeared on the aged glass.

"Christ, it's cold," I whispered, shivering underneath the cloaked bedsheet, wrapping it around me much tighter than before.

Due to my useless watch, and having misplaced my phone, trying to determine the time of day was now impossible. The watch itself wasn't anything special in terms of value, nor was it in any way a collector's piece. It was my father's, and in fact the only item he had left to me before he died. It was a simple watch, accompanied by two (now crinkly) black leather straps that had seen better days. The rear showed my father's faded initials of F.W.

It was an anniversary gift from my mother some years prior to his death. I recalled her telling me that the two letter inscription was all she could afford at the time. No, it was nothing special, but it was sentimental to me and would remain with me, as my father probably would have wanted.

I left the bedroom. The thought of a cosy, blazing fireplace seemed appealing. I made my way down the narrow staircase, almost tripping on the bedsheet that dangled around my feet. Entering the living room, eager to once again feel the pleasurable warmth of the fire, I noticed I'd used the majority of the firewood the previous evening. All of two lonely logs sat on the log store. Hardly enough to keep me warm through the remainder of the day.

I was left with two options. Chopping more firewood or again driving out to the general store to obtain more. I'd seen bundles of firewood on the Café's front porch, sack after sack, towered three times my height.

Why didn't I buy some earlier?

I felt sorry for myself, knowing only too well that both options left me taking on the miserable weather that surrounded the outside world.

The store visit sounded far more to my liking.

But what time is it?

Quickly making my way to the corner of the room. I remembered the grandfather clock was still fully functional.

Impossible, I've completely wasted the day, I thought, letting out a sigh of disappointment. Although I could detect no recognisable fault when I examined the inside, I wondered if its mechanism worked soundly. After all, I wasn't a horologist. *Wait!* A thought occurred, *don't these old things need winding?*

Regardless, through the face of the dusty glass, the grandfather clock displayed the time of five-twenty p.m. What should have only been a short nap had turned into a six-hour coma. I must have needed it. Not once did I stir. One thing now was for certain, I had very little time. With the general store more than likely closed, I was left with no choice but to face a strenuous task in order to rebuild my firewood stock.

Lack of determination had indeed been the best description of my mood. It had been a trying few days. The strangest of days, would be more appropriate. I felt no doubts, however. No regrets necessary for the spontaneous decision that led me here. I stood, listening intently. There was nothing. The day itself was peacefully quiet. *Too quiet,* though this hadn't bothered me. I had grown accustomed to the lack of conversation since my unexpected split with Kate, leaving me with only the gibberish natter of an elderly woman who scuttled about the house. I'd zone out from time to time, ignoring her completely. Oh, how I wish I hadn't done it now. But really! How many times must someone withstand the same ostentatious chatter? Elphin had come to be the life I never expected. A completely inconsistent resemblance to what I once had and knew. I sighed aloud, listening further.

Again, nothing. No people, no cars, no buses or bikes. Not even the relentless bark of a wandering mutt. There was only me. *This really was a lonesome way of living,* I thought. Elphin was a place for the strong, not just of heart, but of mind.

As one arm was placed in the sleeve of my coat, I knew the daylight would soon wither away, and the harsh darkness of the night sky would return.

I stood at the rear doorstep and took a brief moment to adjust to the cold air that struck my nostrils. I trudged through the tall soggy grass to the front of the house to get to the shelter of the storage shed. In my opinion, it reminded me more of a barn, and from its external appearance, could easily fit a tractor or two inside. The door was padlocked. I grasped for the keys inside my inner pocket and slowly rotated them around the keyring, hoping to find one that would match the rusted lock.

"Gotcha," I said with true accomplishment as I removed the padlock from the bracket.

Why is it always the last key?

I eagerly pushed the shed doors that had seized shut. A couple more pushes and they gradually gave way. Inside it was spacious, and to my surprise well-lit. The upper walls were lined with glass panels that rattled in sync with the raw weather. The shed's entire contents were covered in old stained sheets.

A pile of wood was my first and most obvious find. Unfortunately, the logs were far too large to be placed on the grate. An axe would be needed. Before having to investigate further, I happened to spot one, mounted perfectly above the doorframe.

Reaching up and grabbing it, I examined it for purpose.

Odd.

It appeared to be brand-new and recently sharpened, with not a scrape or mark on it. The Letters J.W. were professionally engraved into its handle.

Who engraves an axe?

The rest of the shed housed nothing that piqued my interest. It consisted mainly of gardening equipment, a well-used dining table and chairs, and some old wooden boxes that provided the initials P.D.

For now, the remaining contents weren't important. Picking up the axe and selected logs (that I knew would split easily), I worked through the pile. It was hard going. The weight of the axe taunted my stamina with each inaccurate chop, until my arms grew numb, my mind tired.

Before long, there was a heap of wood that would see me through a couple of nights at least. I gathered them into a stack that would be manageable enough to carry.

Suddenly, the sound of a door slammed. The chopped wood tumbled back to the floor, and I quickly spun round to find the source of the sound. The shed doors remained sturdy in their place.

Maybe something had blown over, or it may have been a vehicle passing by.

I gathered the logs back into my arms and started the walk back to the cottage.

SLAM.

The noise struck again. I stopped. The sound hit me just as intensely as it had the first time. I strode out of the wooden building, expecting nothing more than a reasonable explanation. Again, the logs dropped to the ground, several hit my feet, and rolled farther down the driveway. The front door was now clearly wide open, but I had no explanation as to why or how.

Echoes of Home

Chapter Fourteen

The door itself had remained locked since my arrival, with no trace of any key in sight. No movement appeared from the inside windows; no indication of a passer-by appeared evident either. Still I felt so strongly that an invasion of the property had been made.

Almost stumbling amongst the logs that lay at my feet, I quickly walked to the door, my focus never once parting from the open entry. The empty hallway and staircase remained perfectly visible though isolated.

Not bothering to question whether I should call out to any trespassers that could in fact be sneaking around the house, I yelled, "Who's there?"

My voice sounded weak and helpless. I hurried back to the wooden hut and picked up the axe. Holding it tightly in both hands, I returned to the opening of the cottage.

"I have a weapon, come out now, and…and I won't swing for you." My statement came across much stronger than the last I spoke. I looked down to my weapon, the rain rebounding from its steel head.

Would I really cause harm to another person?

At this time, I dare say I would, only insecurity clouded my state of mind. Of course, there was no reply from my demanding statement, I never expected there to be. But at that time, I couldn't be sure if that was good news or bad. Either way, I had no choice. I would need to search the cottage carefully.

There was no need to examine the door itself. There appeared to be no form of forced entry. Neither was any key in place to suggest someone had unlocked it to gain access.

I searched that cottage from top to bottom that day, all the while, never letting go of my trusty axe that could, without question, shatter the life of another. The kitchen, the bedrooms, the bathroom, the lounge, all of them displayed nothing more than settled dust and a deadly silence.

Now more at ease than before, I slackened my grip, and the axe now rested at my side as the door continued to swing. There was no one, not a soul.

I continued with collecting the logs that still lay scattered on the driveway, returning back into the house. The more trips that were made, the more comfortable and confident I became. Nothing, no, nothing was now out of the ordinary.

With the wooden storage hut once again locked tight, I keenly retreated inside, bolting the keyless front door behind me.

The fire was soon alive and heated the room as promptly as before, and I took rest on the chair in front of the blaze, but only for a short time, listening to the wind as it whistled and swirled down the funnel of the stone chimney.

The room across from the living area still remained firmly closed. It wasn't until now the strong desire and impatient need to unlock this secret room took hold of me. Without haste or regret I stood, firmly jiggling the door handle before back-pacing to collect the axe.

Chapter Fifteen

The door lay scattered in pieces across the floor. My breathless, uncontrollable wheezing was evident as I peered into the vacant mystery of the room. I stepped forward, surprised with my discovery.

The room, in fact, offered nothing to marvel upon at all. No beds, no chairs, no units, no carpet, no decoration nor light switch, for that matter. It was a room of emptiness. A room in which I could imagine no past happiness or warmth.

Covering my mouth with my one free hand, I attempted to prevent taking back the years of settled dust and dampening smell. I took a few more steps forward for closer inspection, yet still nothing of interest was viewed at that present time.

The wall directly in front of me showed the outline of what once was a small, narrow window, now boarded up with a mixture of slatted panels. These planks had been fixed to the wall, giving a slight impression of panic in its hanging crisscross effect. There was nothing more to see, nothing more to inspect.

Exiting, I picked up the few remaining broken pieces of the door that I knew would continue to feed the fire as I rested in a breathless state.

The clock behind me struck six-thirty. I had allowed the fire to die down, which left me with a remaining fifteen logs to be burnt throughout the monotonous evening. Slightly fatigued and my time unoccupied, I inquisitively searched through several of the old unit drawers in a hopeful attempt to find something that could possibly pique my interest. Most of the units hid nothing more than old papers, books, and trinket boxes.

If my memory serves me correctly, it was on the second shelf of the third unit that I noticed an interesting piece of paper.

It was a photograph. A photograph that resembled the house I now lived in.

The photograph was old, colourless, and appeared slightly blurred at first glance. Time had given the vintage picture a collected layer of dust that I gently brushed away to study its image intently. It was indeed Elphin Cottage. The picture remained faded, despite the dust being well removed, I held it under the brightness of a glowing table lamp.

I studied it carefully. It was clearly taken from the driveway. Two young gentlemen in suits were visible, their stance straight, staring into the camera lens. Both their faces cast blank expressions as the cottage stood beautiful and proud in the background. A small stone plaque rested at their feet. The inscription on the plaque was near impossible to read and provided very little more to be studied.

The photo was left abandoned on the table as the evening refreshments of tinned soup and a plate of butter-less bread was prepared. I sat comfortably in front of the fire, the hot bowl of soup balanced carefully on my lap. The sound of the steel spoon hitting the dish echoed about the room like the toll of a bell. Once finished, I allowed my head to slowly rest back. I closed my eyes and breathed deeply, satisfied that another day had come to a close.

Then my heart froze as it began all over again. The attention-seeking tapping bounced around the room once more. Again and again, the tapping continued as if on glass. Circling the room with my gaze gave me no indication or guidance of its true source.

I stood quickly, eagerly, checking just as I did only the night before. Though the more I searched, the more aggravated the tapping became. Without hesitation, I fled from the room, unbolting the front door and lunging into the darkness, without thought of who might be loitering there.

The night was still and silent. No breeze brushed past me, only the coldness of the air surrounded my skin. I shivered intently.

Now there was silence. The sound of pebbles crushed beneath my feet with each and every step was all that could be heard. Looking back at the house and the glowing window of the room I had just abandoned, I considered my options and slowly walked back to the front door.

No presence appeared in the cramped hallway, nor was there any sound that paraded through my ears as I strode down the lightless corridor, desperate to reach the glow of the living room light. I peered into the room. Nothing stirred. No item to my knowledge was moved or misplaced.

And now no noise was present at all. The fire still burned brightly, sending floating embers shooting up the chimney, throwing out that same comforting warmth. Despite the waving heat, I still shivered viciously from the time I'd spent outdoors.

Sitting, I held my hands out in front of the flames in an attempt to cure the chill. It was then a distant light flickered at the corner of my eye. It actually took a moment for the intermittent flicking to grab my full attention. As I turned, the light guided me beyond the planks of wood that remained nailed against the unoccupied room's window.

I uneasily re-entered the room, and the light continued to flicker as I peered through the narrow gaps of the planks. The swaying light was visible, but its source still remained unknown. With uncertainty, I gripped one of the planks to remove it. To my surprise, it came completely loose from the nailed position. The plank dropped firmly to the floor with a hollow clatter.

It now became clear to me that the flickering light came from the cottage that sat across the moor from my own. Little else was visible from where I stood, as the dusty planks and dirt-sprayed window restricted my view.

Deciding to get a closer look, I hurried down the hall and out through the door, this time not forgetting to wrap up warm. I threw my coat over my shoulders to defeat the harsh weather. Visibility was poor, and I stumbled several times, trying not to repeat the previous fall. I arched my neck to the evening sky which displayed thousands of beautifully shining stars that illuminated the night. I'd never seen anything quite like it in my life.

Coming to a halt, I viewed the far distance, searching for the cottage that had caused me to vacate my lodging. No flickering light now appeared, only the glowing beams of the stars existed above me. Nothing but darkness covered the mountains and vast landscape.

As I listened intently for voices, the only sound was the rippling Ledmore river that made itself known ahead. I had no intention to stay and wait. This whole situation was becoming an irritating joke. The noises inside the old house, the expressionless white figure, and now the intermittent lights that appeared on the land across from the cottage.

Taking a step inside, I allowed myself a hot beverage that would hopefully shake off the cold and fell back into the armchair, trying at best to regain my senses. I brushed both hands through my hair and rested back, drifting into a deep sleep accompanied by an uncomfortable terror that surrounded my dreams.

Chapter Sixteen

*C*oldness surrounded me, so cold I found myself frozen in the position where I knelt, wearing nothing but ragged clothing. I grabbed my arms, rubbing them furiously in hope to feel warmth.

My uncared-for clothes displayed holes and patches, my shirt torn and thin, my trousers shredded from the knees down.

Sadness clouded my mind. I pleaded and prayed for warmth, but no warmth came as I stayed kneeling on the ground. I felt the sensation of snow as it softly landed all over my shivering, exposed skin, and despite looking to the stars, all that could be seen was darkness.

Using all the energy I could muster, I stood. Pain flourished over my body. My feet were numb and somehow bleeding. The ground lay thick with smog so dense that nothing could be seen. The sound of snow crushing underfoot filled the air, and each step sent sharp, painful jolts between my already wounded toes.

I staggered through the darkness, the coldness pushing me to the ground again and again. With each fall, my skin more sharply stung as though trying to shatter. I held my shaking hands in front of my face to protect my crying eyes.

The far distance faintly displayed a cottage, all the windows alight. A wheezy breathlessness dominated my lungs as I tried to trudge through the harsh terrain, the cottage getting closer with each and every stumble.

The darkened shape of the stone building now finally became clearer. I rested on the porch beside the door, frantically struggling to regain my breath. I reached out, stretching for the door handle that, when turned, remained stiffly in its place.

"No, not locked, not locked, please, God, open,"

I pleaded, continually attempting to twist the unyielding handle, now banging on the sturdy wood, determined to be heard by its occupier. My blistered hands stung with each and every thud, but still, no one answered my cries.

Lights glowed warmly through the small boxed windows, situated on both sides of the house. I stumbled, my hands resting on the stone wall, supporting my body as each struggling step brought me closer to the bright internal light.

I peered inside. There were still figures present. Both my palms smothered the surface of the glass, displaying faint smeared streaks of blood from my wounded fingers. I shouted frantically with every ounce of energy that remained within me, until nothing more than a broken crackle of cries seeped past my lips. Still the figures remained unmoved. No reaction was made to my presence. Neither did any amount of pleading or slamming create a distraction to the many figures that stood silently inside, their backs still faced my whimpering cries for help.

Intense pain from the cold now pushed me back to the ground.

"There's no room for you here," a faintly gruff voice yelled out, almost non-existent through the howling wind.

I looked about myself desperately to find the source of the voice.

Crawling to the door again, I huddled on the porch step, burying my face into my knees.

Again, the same voice yelled out, "There's nothing for you here."

With one hand, I continued to knock on the door, until each knock became limper and my cries turned only to whispers. The call of tiredness swept through my already drained body. All sensations suddenly died. No longer did I feel pain, only the sense of numbness remained. A daze clouded my mind and sight. My knocking halted, and both hands now stilled as snow settled on my curled-up knees.

"I'm going to die," I whispered, diverting my head that now sank between my quivering knees. I felt faint, on the verge of blacking out. And as I rested, I brought my head up one last time to gaze on the darkened world before I slipped away.

My vision blurred, all life escaping me. And before all went black, my head tilted slowly to the side. In view was a small girl huddled beside me, she, too, freezing to death.

I awoke in a panicked state, soon realising my surroundings. I hunched forward retching, attempting to recollect the memory of such a vivid dream. After several minutes of trying to convince myself of the fictional events, the grandfather clock struck one-thirty. The fire had once again turned to ash, and the bitter chill of the room reformed its presence.

I'd never dreamt in such a way before. It all seemed so clear…so real, as though the terror I experienced had become a true reality.

Standing, my heart thumping mightily, I shook off the unpleasant cold that without doubt was a likely factor to my disturbed sleep.

The old photograph still lay on the table, and I picked it up once more for yet another inspection. Something caught me about the fading image, a familiar sense one could say. A sudden delayed realisation hit me as I studied the image further.

"How did I not see it?" I said with disbelief.

My committed attention now focused solely on the man to the right in the picture. This was a man I already knew. Despite the ageing of the photo, it became clear to me that the man was without a doubt a gentleman I had met earlier that day.

This was unmistakably an image of Mr Coull's past self.

Echoes of Home

Chapter Seventeen

The very next morning, I decided to make an early start, wanting some answers. The distant cottage was as good a place as any to start. I packed a small lunchbox, its contents including a wedge of cheese from the fridge that by now proved to keep supplies more tepid than cool. The rest contained two slices of buttered bread and a large helping of biscuits. And for a beverage, I filled a tall Thermos with hot lemon tea and placed it into the side compartment of a shoulder bag.

Making sure I dressed appropriately for the weather conditions, I wrapped myself in multiple layers of clothing, laced my boots tightly, then stepped out of the house. The car would not be needed on this day. I brushed my hand on its bonnet as I walked down the driveway path in the direction of the Ledmore river.

It wasn't long before my easy stroll on Highland paths turned to extremely rough terrain. Long grass curled and tangled round my feet, and I fell several times to the soft padded ground. Vibrant green moss that expanded over the land sent me stumbling off balance, my weight compressing the greenery to the soil.

The day was bright, and although the sun peeked through the clouds, a morning frost still spread across the ground, twinkling in reflection to the light of the sky.

I quickened my steps, hopping over the scattered moss patches to reach the levelled terrain. Pushing through a cluster of small trees, the edge of the river soon came into view. With need of crossing, I studied the naturally flowing water. No easy access points to cross appeared visible to me at the time. The rippling water, although not overly deep, could be waded across easily enough by foot, if you were in the right mind to get a little wet. Unfortunately, I was not. But what choice did I have in the matter?

Very much needing to cross, I crouched and rested on the mossy bank, removing both boots and placing them into the top compartment of my bag, followed by my thick woollen socks.

My trousers were turned up to the knees, and I hesitatingly dipped my left foot first into the clear-flowing river.

"Jesus, that's cold." I screeched, intently biting my bottom lip.

Soon, my right foot was given the same tortuous treatment, and I carefully waded through the river. At second glance, the water's depth was more than I initially anticipated. The flow hit the top of my knees, and with each step, its force attempted to push me farther downstream.

Once at the other side of the bank, my body had already adjusted to the low temperature. With my feet now slightly numb, I stepped up onto the grassy bank, allowing my skin to air dry in the soft morning breeze.

The inclined bank was certainly steeper than I imagined. Each step upwards became more exhausting than the last, my knees buckling with tiredness, my body fatigued. I pushed consistently to reach my goal ahead, stopping to rest beside a half-fallen tree.

I scouted the land in front of me, admiring the scenery of my own land in the distance. I poured myself half a cup of tea, the zesty taste helping me regain my strength. The thermos was again safely tucked into the side compartment of the bag as I peered up at the intimidating hillside before me.

A chimney peaked just over the edge of the hill crest. For a brief moment, the sun escaped the clouds, shining down on me as I looked to the sky above. The warm sensation was short-lived. The light soon became surrounded by thick, dull cloud that dominated the sky and the land below. A narrow flowing stream dashed its way down the hillside, visibly feeding into the Ledmore river at its surface.

Leaping over the inclined stream brought me a little closer to the cottage. The wind blew much stronger now, whistling through the leafless trees. The cottage now stood in view. A small bird flew up from the grounds, shrieking, as if to alarm the area of my presence.

From the side view, the cottage itself seemed in need of major repair. Tiles that I'm sure once rested proudly on its roof now lay scattered and shattered on the moss-covered ground. The front of the cottage hardly improved. Glass windows hung desperately, partly smashed in their frames, the door visibly rotting away as it swiftly swung from side to side in response to the breeze. A rusty lantern hung by the side of the door.

Without doubt, this would be the light source that had caught my attention only the previous evening. It came to me, while I surveyed the front of the grounds, that not one path led to the retired dwelling. It was clearly evident that it had been cut off from the rest of the world, and for many years.

It was at that moment, I noticed how quiet the vast surroundings had become around me. No longer did the wind howl, forcefully shaking the trees. No longer did birds glide and screech, informing me of my trespass on their lands.

The silence disturbed my train of thought. The man who was so eager to investigate the inside of this stone building now appeared hesitant of what he might find. Before continuing, I waited impatiently for the wind to display its forcefulness and the wildlife to show their existence once more.

Chapter Eighteen

T he same lingering silence persisted. A shallow creak caught my attention as the rotting door slowly groaned on its hinges. My right hand now on the door, I pushed slightly forward, giving me the full entrance of the cottage.

On first impression, it was clear to see the building hadn't been lived in for an extremely long time. Nothing occupied its small rectangular space other than animals when in desperate need of shelter. Droppings spread across the dirt-covered floor.

It astounded me to think that once this two-roomed cottage would have served as a family home. Another thought occurred, I wondered why its owners had left, leaving the place they called home to wither and ruin over time.

Any light that aided me shone narrowly through the roof's gaps, where the slate tiles no longer lay. One thing, however, was evident: the fireplace and chimney were still structurally well intact. Further to that, they clearly served a purpose not too long ago. Half-burned logs and fresh black ash lay mounted inside its arch.

Possibly a hiker eager to seek refuge from a storm.

Or was this the doing of children up to no good? If that were the case, they could hardly be blamed. There wasn't exactly much here to occupy the younger generation's mind.

A violent smash had me jumping from my skin, and instinct had me running to the door under the impression that harm was about to befall me. I peeked around the corner, and the smash struck again. Though my panic was soon brought to a halt as I watched a further three roof tiles slip from position and shatter into pieces on the floor.

A slight sigh of relief escaped me, followed by a short chuckle at my own embarrassment. I took one last look at the ruin then circled its grounds. Looking for something. What that was, I wasn't sure.

Two small stone cairns were located at the rear far side of the cottage, now surrounded by the overgrown grass. Each stone cairn ran alongside the crumbling external wall, both no more than a quarter of a metre in height. The piled rocks now lay in a disorganised fashion.

A couple of smooth-surfaced stones sat at my feet, that I picked up and added to the top of each pile. Why I added these further stones I was unsure. Maybe it was just to prove my existence, as so many others had done before me.

The isolated land around me remained deathly still, giving one the slight suspicion of being watched. I sat, leaning against the crumbling wall, imagining what life must have been like here so long ago, and wondered about the endless stories that seeped from its crumbling walls. Although the atmosphere had not changed, there was something extremely peaceful about its location. I couldn't quite put my finger on it. It gave off the strong impression that the people who once lived here were happy and content in life, unburdened by the rat race of life we have today, their only true concern to look out for their loved ones and enjoy the pleasure of the surrounding lands.

I wonder what caused the beginning of the end for such a place.

Regaining my stance, and collecting my bag, I decided to descend. There was nothing more to see here.

I returned at a steady pace, and the atmosphere of the land suddenly appeared to come back to life. The noise of the rushing water was now vacantly burbling in the distance, and as I trudged down the steep terrain, the breeze gradually regained its strength, refreshingly cooling the sweat from my brow.

At one point, I paused and turned to look back. The cottage now appeared near invisible to the world, its grey stone only slightly viewable through the cluster of thick branches.

Finally, I hit level ground, arriving back at the rushing river. I sat on the bank, taking in the peaceful sounds of nature and the rippling water, tucking in to my prepared lunch.

I finished the remainder of my lemon tea and watched a dozen fish spring to the surface of the water, eagerly hunting the breadcrumbs I had thrown in from the side of the bank. Again, it was time to face the chill. So, I rolled up my trousers to repeat my stride across the river.

By the time I finally reached the garden drive, the morning had well and truly passed. The small stone plaque which was displayed on the faded image I found only the previous day was now clearly visible as I strolled along the path. Cutting my way across the untended garden, I stood directly above the plaque, then knelt, moving the grass aside in order to study its words.

Elphin Cottage
A saviour to the hearts of the land.
Protector of the Great storm.
20/02/1847
Le ùine thoir mathanas don pheacadh again.

This house was indeed older than my expectations. Elphin Cottage had stood its test of time, unlike the mimic of a cottage I previously visited that morning. The event and date meant nothing to me. Neither did the final sentence engraved across the bottom. Moments later, I attended that same plaque, writing down on paper, word for word, the inscription displayed in gold-plated writing.

Folding the paper and placing it into my back pocket, I held out the old photograph brought from the house, comparing its likeness to the plaque below me.

Its writing was a mystery to me, yet I needed – no, wanted – more information. One of the men depicted in this photograph I knew was still local.

Where would I find him now?

*

For the next several days, I tried multiple stores and farmhouses, calling at lodgings uninvited in an attempt to source Mr Coull's location. With me being relatively new to the area, many folks stood on guard. In some cases, they even ignored me when I tried to gain answers that, in their eyes, were no business of mine. On my third attempt to gain knowledge from the local café, they finally allowed me to leave a message, just in case the man happened to arrive at any point in the upcoming days. Mr Coull was certainly a difficult one to track, but I was determined to find the man who stood faded on the photograph I possessed.

I spent one particular day at the location of Ullapool, a town only a short distance away from my humble cottage in Elphin. But still, it was satisfying to walk amongst a busier community than my own.

The small town sat at the bank's edge of Loch Broom, an impressively large loch that fed directly to the sea. Sitting at its bank, I watched as the fishing boats lazily sailed out of their ports, starting their hard day's work ahead.

It was particularly cold that morning. A low mist hovered over the water, disturbed only by the creatures that resided within. A fisherman stood lonely on its shore, patiently casting his rod into the thinly layered mist.

I sat watching the man for some time, endlessly trying to catch a bite. He was greeted only by a seal, curiously popping its head from the misty water. Several times more, the man cast out his line, the seal approaching closer to him with each and every throw. He soon walked onto another spot, defeated by the mammal that now rested on the shore.

I walked along a path of Ullapool's town that afternoon, taking in its meek heritage sights. I casually people-watched, eating some hot salty chips while walking. Near the end of the path, on the outskirts of town, there stood a small stone monument surrounded by tiny vibrant flowers. The monument itself was reasonably maintained.

Its writing stated:

Remembering the lives that had passed during the building of Destitution Road.

Again, this was another event that meant nothing to me. The learning of any Scottish history was virtually non-existent during my education years, despite my interest in such topics. I decided to collect a small pamphlet from the tourist information centre before returning to the car.

The car fired up the first time, a surprise considering that for the past few days its engine needed a little more convincing than usual. It was late afternoon but in no way near to sunset. Having no desire to go home, I drove farther north for the first time since arriving.

It took roughly an hour before reaching familiar territory. The same Elphin Café swung into view from the hillside, shortly followed by the cottage some miles later. Not exactly sure of where I was heading, I continued to drive past the cottage. Without doubt, the direction would lead to more bewildering Highland roads.

I drove alongside the house, catching a glimpse of the ruined cottage that stood in the distance. This time, however, I paid it no further attention.

Chapter Nineteen

The road twisted and twined, opening up hidden secrets as further beautiful landscapes burst into view. It was true what they say, difficult roads certainly lead to beautiful destinations. I looked upon the valleys. Intermittent bursts of sunlight shone fluently through the clouds, shining on the distant land below, giving its location a touch of magic as I passed.

It wasn't much farther until my tour of the lands came to a halt. A gentleman stood alone to the side of the road, a frantic waving gesture made in my direction. Clearly, he insisted I immediately pull over.

It was an elderly gentleman, at first guess around his late seventies. He had an extremely poor posture, his back hunched over as he reached out one hand to a collapsing wooden fence.

Pulling over, I dropped the passenger window down to enquire if any assistance was needed for him.

Maybe he injured himself in some way.

"Is all okay?" I asked.

He slowly approached the vehicle. "Nay, I'm fine as it goes, but it would be wise not to drive through here, my friend."

He was softly spoken, presenting a gaunt, confused expression on his wrinkled face, as if confusion clouded his mind.

"Oh, I see, sir, why is that?"

He peered through the window, his head almost reaching the interior of the car. "The river only a mile down has burst its banks. Wouldn't be a particularly good idea to go driving that way, son. I'm just waiting until the authorities arrive to post the hazard. Goodness knows when that will be!"

I frowned, feeling slightly sorry for the frail figure who waited for help.

"Are the authorities aware?" I asked with concern for the old man's welfare.

"Oh, yes, boy, yes. Although I couldn't say when they'll arrive. No one seems to rush to get to these parts." He paused a second. "Saying that, son, I'd stand here all night if there was a chance it could prevent with someone getting into a spot of trouble."

"Indeed," I replied with a nod of appreciation.

Now with very little left in terms of conversation, placing his hand on the roof, he bent further to gain better sight of me. A concerned look on his face. "Best get yourself home, son, it's gonnae be a rough evening. Giving out one hell of a storm, so they say. The worst this year, so I believe."

Unaware of any storm, I thought it only right to enquire further. "A storm…when? This evening, you say?"

"Yes, son, we get them regular enough during this time of year. Many folk just get used to it. We can deal with the regular heavy rains in these parts, but when snow starts fallin'…well, that's a different matter entirely."

"How bad is it expected to be?" I questioned, with more interest in my voice.

"Hmmm, hard to say, my friend, hard to say. It varies. Last year we had similar warnings. The snow caused damage to several of the local's houses, not to mention closure to many of the roads in the area. I'd say it can make an already isolated place far more challenging."

Looking to the sky, I only saw blue with the scattered grey cloud. "I had no idea." I was now concerned about my own welfare.

The gentleman asked me where I was located, and once I explained to him that I was far more local than he expected, he held out his hand and shook mine weakly.

"Listen, son, if you find things get a little too rough, go to the Inn"

"The Inn?" I repeated inquisitively.

"Yes, son, the Inn. It's called the Dram Inn, to be more accurate. As a community, we try and help some folk by organising a safety point during such weather. It's comfort to those who live alone, and it keeps the local bar owner happy to gain a little further income during such a peak time. If in any bother, son, please go there."

The frail man spent the next few minutes attempting to explain the location of the Inn, which seemed to be only a brisk forty-five minute walk from my doorstep. I thanked him for his help, and he made a simple nodding gesture in return.

I turned the car around and carefully drove towards home, acknowledging him as I left.

He held up his hand, shouting, "Stay safe, son, stay safe."

I looked into the rear-view mirror, and the frail man had shrunk in size, never moving from his position, until his figure fell from view.

By the time I returned to the cottage, heavy clouds had already appeared from the west. Within a short space of time, the thick, dull greenish grey hung overhead, controlling the sky above. The few upcoming hours would consist of making preparations for the forthcoming weather. I had little knowledge of how to prepare or what to expect. For some reason, it caused a brief case of anxiety.

I gave myself a moment to calm my nerves. The feeling soon eased, and I was able to continue with preparing for the event ahead.

Food in the kitchen was scarce, but now I was left with no time to visit the local store and restock my provisions. What food I had would simply have to do. I spent some time restocking the log store inside the house, making multiple trips to and from the storage shed. Being over cautious didn't seem to cause me concern, and making sure there was enough wood to keep the fire glowing brightly throughout the night could be my only comfort.

I removed the old dining table, and my car was soon placed inside the barn that would hopefully protect it from the harsh elements forecast. Now, as prepared as I could be and not knowing what exactly to expect, I waited inside, peering out as the storm gradually brewed.

Echoes of Home

Chapter Twenty

Slowly but surely, the weather stirred. The once gentle breeze now howled with each intermittent gust, tree branches abruptly rocking from side to side in a continuous motion. Soon, the wind grew so powerful it was attacking the house. The windows and external doors vigorously rattled on their hinges, almost as though forced entry was at that moment being attempted.

For a brief moment, the same anxious feeling once again took hold of me. I could do nothing more than wait, staring at the forceful weather that surrounded the Highlands.

Allowing myself to take a break from my window's side view, I sat uneasy, hoping, wishing that the current weather would be the worst to come. I was proven wrong. By the time the clock stuck six forty-five, the first snow fell harshly, sticking to the ground almost instantly. Any light that attempted to seep through the sky's white blanket was bound to fail. Daylight had now passed.

The dominating mountains in the distance now became invisible to the human eye, and soon the nearer land, too, disappeared from sight. I sat in the chair, my eyes kept closed, only enhancing the sound of the brutal weather outside. To my side, on the coffee table, lay the old photograph of the cottage and its two figures. Picking up the image, I held it with care under the lamp's light.

Blackness then engulfed the room. The lamps flickered aggressively, then darkness surrounded my space. I hoped power to the house would immediately resume, but unfortunately, it did not.

It was odd, but as I now sat in the darkened room, the storm appeared to be even more furious than before. Attempting to power the house turned to failure as I stumbled through the blackened, suffocating rooms, my anxiety involuntarily hitting its peak.

Inside the living room I again sat, eager to strike a fire on the grate. It only took a moment but felt as though it was an eternity. The fire now spat and popped as air escaped the kiln wood. I waited in silence for the fire to completely take hold, sending flickering shadows onto the walls of the chimney breast. I continued to sit there, on guard, desperate to keep my only light source from fading.

Maybe this had been a huge mistake? I needed a fresh start; I knew that much. However, I hadn't considered the consequences of what my action would bear. I wished to be alone. I made peace with such matters. So, why did I hate the sense of loneliness? *Is there a difference?* I questioned. But I was far too weary to reflect further.

I felt so hungry, my stomach churning for the want of only food. I looked about me, not knowing where at all I was. A small enclosed room surrounded me, its ground filthy, its windows boarded solidly in place.

"Food... I need food," I called out.

The cramping tightened further around my sunken belly, my body curling into the floor for protection. The dirt from it embedded its way deep into my fingernails as I grasped the floor for aid. My stomach felt as though it was a rope, continually twisting until the knot at its centre could take no more. I gasped for relief, letting out a scream from its torture.

A sharp cramp shooting up my neck awoke me. The fire still burned bright, and I could tell without looking that the weather was still as persistent as before.

What a horrible dream, I thought through the discomfort clenching firmly at the back of my tender neck.

I stood, slightly off balance, narrowing my eyes to catch the time displayed. It was then as I turned, a flicker of light flashed in the opposite direction. It became immediately clear that the light source shone through the planks of wood, still hung nailed to the window of the empty room.

I panted in the dust-filled air, my heartbeat thumping inside my ears. As I focused my vision again through the large gap of the wooden boards, it became clear instantly. As expected, the light source was the distant lantern, violently swinging back and forth in the location of the ruined cottage on the hill.

Did my eyes deceive me?

No, after first glance, my senses appeared perfectly reliable. The more I focused, the more I saw that very same lantern shake from side to side. One thing was now certain, I again wanted a closer look.

Grabbing my coat, I trudged my way through the still darkened house and unbolted the front door. What hit me was the sharpness of the weather. With each gust, the snow continuously struck my face. No matter how I tried to conceal myself, the snow swept through, and with it, the feeling of tiny razors striking my flesh. I forced myself forward into the blistering cold and, cowering under the hood of my coat, I continued to stagger, finally reaching the end of the driveway.

There I stood. My squinted eyes strained through the harsh weather to the site of the lantern, its glow now appearing even more intense than before. Nothing more could be seen of the surrounding land, the snow had seen to that.

Deciding to take on the cold in the first place now seemed like nothing more than an unpleasant mistake. Again, shielding my already stinging nose, I turned and headed back towards the house.

Stupidly, I'd left the door fully open. On my approach, a thin layer of white snow had already blown its way in, covering the inside of the hallway with an icy layer.

I closed the door behind me with a forceful push, and it sent me immediately falling to the slate floor. My boots slipped on the icy surface, and with each attempt to regain my stance, I stumbled further. I regained my posture and held the walls firmly for guidance. And as I walked back to my chair, the interior of the house continued to darken as the night sky gradually set in for the evening.

The fire was fully ablaze, not at all how I remembered it. When I had left, its appearance was weakening. Although now the flames danced frantically with endless life. The room itself pushed against me with warmth upon entering, and my intense shaking faltered almost instantly.

Had I fuelled the grate before I left?

I couldn't quite remember. Maybe I had. But I was too grateful for the satisfying warmth to care further. I sat hunched, my hands out to the flames. My mindset had calmed, for now. As I rested back on the leather chair, my head lay tilted to its side, eyes closed. My breathing slowed, and I listened to the sounds of the harmful storm.

It was then I opened my eyes to the sight of a hand pressed up against the glass of the window. I leaned forward in fright, not moving from the seat. The hand lay flat, its palm smothered with scrapes and cuts.

With no sudden movement, I slowly stood to my feet, and as I did, the hand slid down the wet pane, creating a squeal in its path. Once it finally reached the edge of the pane, it removed itself from sight.

Only the blackness of the window was present, not even my own reflection appeared to tease my sanity. I waited frightfully for the hand to reappear.

Had it been real? Or did my state of mind portray such further trickery?

There was no point questioning myself. The smudge of the handprint that remained was perfectly observable. And with that print, drops of blood lay stained on the glass surface.

Did someone need help? A local seeking aid and shelter, or was I seeing what purely should not be?

I never entertained the idea of ghouls and goblins, yet some experiences since my arrival defied reasonable explanation. My back pressing against the wall, I peeked past the side of the window, hoping to find the soul who rested below its ledge. No one could be seen, or heard for that matter. My heart thumped, the hairs on my neck standing on patrol.

I walked away hesitantly, but then the hand appeared again, its palm slamming flat against the glass with an horrendous crash, instantly sliding down out of view. The same motion repeated several times more before I fled the room.

Grabbing my keys in utter panic, I abandoned the house without regret in order to escape the noises and sights around me.

Chapter Twenty-One

Foggy breath clouded my sight. The sound of my panting roared with panic. I sprinted from the porch. Again, I struggled with the keys to the storage shed. For that short time, I didn't feel the cold. Only adrenaline coursed rapidly through my veins. I struck lucky. On the third key, the lock unbolted. The double doors immediately swung open with force.

The car sat peacefully. Its glass not yet bitten from harsh frost. Without the use of a seatbelt, I fired up its engine, and the car jolted forward from its place. Its wheels spun frantically through the first layer of mounted snow, and little progress was made between me and the house. Soon, I slowly found myself at a halt, sitting only a yard or two from the cottage.

"Come on, move!" I shouted, pressing excessively on the pedal, desperately wanting to make distance.

Its tyres continued to spin like a hamster wheel, grinding the snow layers down until hitting the surface of icy ground. The more I cursed and yelled, the more my position remained idle. The thought of something holding me back, denying me to flee, engaged my mind. The feeling didn't let up until I stepped out of the car and the sound of the struggling engine was behind me. Steam quickly exuded from its bonnet.

I turned to view the window. The hand that aggressively slammed against its glass now ceased to exist, and after a quick observation, neither did the bloody smudge marks or prints. In fact, the light again shone brightly in the room.

But I wouldn't return inside, not tonight. Not after what I had just witnessed. What started as suspicion now seemed so real. The fear I had experienced was real.

I'm sure of it.

I attempted to move the car only once more, pushing on the rear, hoping it would somehow budge from its place. There was no point in attempting again. With the snow lying thick along the driveway, it would only be a matter of time before I ran aground.

Taking the keys from the ignition, I abandoned the car and scurried by foot down to the entrance gate. Hanging on to its iron bars, I stopped to catch my breath, then dared to look back. Electricity once again fed into the house. The lights from the rooms shone brightly, illuminating the darkness, almost as if it were a point of safety for anyone endangered by the surrounding area.

I altered my stance to look forward. The lantern swinging from the ruined cottage also beamed a blinding ray of light, it, too, a beacon to the land. But the more I observed, the more its light became faint. Now only darkness engulfed its glimmer.

I won't go back there.

The words repeated around my head, time and time again. The Inn the old gentleman advised me of wasn't too far, and to be honest, I was sure I could make it, despite the weather. As long as I kept a steady pace.

Holding on to the gate no longer, I thrust forward, headfirst, into a gale of snow, never once looking back behind me.

I hiked along the road for some time, each step almost catching me further off balance than the last. The twisted road opened up into flatter land soon enough. The gale winds pushed me from side to side, and snow continued to effortlessly hammer its way to the ground. The cold swept its way into my bones, my legs aching, and my chest stiffening.

It wasn't too long before my feet were soaking. With every step, they buried through the icy surface, snow invading my boots. A small bridge came into view farther up the road. I had travelled over it that very afternoon, the Ledmore river flowing steadily beneath.

When at last I reached its dry, stone structure, I sought refuge for a short time under its wall. Luckily, there was a small lump of land beneath the bridge that remained dry, untouched by the aggressive snowfall.

I bent my knees, my back flat against the wall's arch. The river's sound burbled continuously past in the darkness, its rippling pattern somewhat comforting to the mind.

Rubbing my hands together for warmth, I closed my eyes tightly shut, listening intently to the whine of the wind as it flew briskly through the small tunnel.

I needed to move. If I didn't, I would undoubtedly freeze to death. Despite the uneasy thought, I still remained where I sat for a little while longer, only encouraging myself to make haste. Thanks to cover, the stinging in my face had subsided. My hands had gained warmth, as I'd buried them deep into my pockets, but my feet were still fighting the bitter chill that now presented a sensation of numbness on each and every toe.

I stood, my knee joints aching from where I'd sat curled. The snow still fell from the heavens, but the wind had eased. I needed no further persuasion. It was time to move.

The walk now seemed ten times harder than before. The darkened lands before me displayed only vast white mounds. Even the road itself was no longer identifiable, camouflaged by the falling clumps of ice. From memory, I knew the road would soon make a left at some point, but from where proved to be impossible to tell. A huddle of shadowed wood nestled boldly to my left. That seemed a much shorter distance to cut through in the long run.

Not really considering my actions, I headed in the direction of the wood. Attempting to quicken my pace, I breathed heavily, the wheeze from my chest whistling into the night air. A small, almost invisible barbed wire fence struck my stride. I rebounded from its wires, grazing my thigh in the process. Frustrated by my own lack of awareness, I kicked the snow-bound ground, attempting to venture over the obstacle.

The fence had seen better days. Its posts had rotted from the ground, displaying only the tense wire to stop it from falling. By my pushing one of the upright posts, the fence soon tilted, enabling me to easily climb over its rickety structure uninjured. The woodland, although shadowed, was clearly approaching, and the closer its shape became in appearance, the harder my legs pushed on the slippery ground.

Reaching the wood's edge, I rested, falling against the first tree I stumbled upon. The wall of pine trees stood high, their branches sprouted thickly overhead, allowing minimal light to reach the surface. The snow still managed to find its way past the trees' scattered arms, displaying as only a gentle flurry through the air.

I stepped past the first set of trees, and the wind suddenly silenced. Its only evidence was the noise of branches rustling and swaying above me. Regardless of my hopes, there appeared to be nothing but endless trees for as far as the eye could see.

My pace eased. I was much more relaxed and less exposed, and although the cold still surrounded my body, the army of trees blocked the harshness of the breeze. All was so quiet. The sound of my boots crunching through the snow dominated the silent space. Intermittently, the crunch of twigs snapped beneath my feet, its echo reflecting back at me from the far distance.

There was no other sign of life out here on such a night. No graceful stags pranced throughout the tree trunks. No shrieking birds were heard from the safety of their nests. I was the only soul foolish enough to walk amongst the elements. The creatures of the land had vanished, seeking refuge, patiently waiting for the storm to pass.

I leaned forward to again catch my breath. The uneven ground inclined slightly, my legs shaking and throbbing. Tired, hungry, and in desperate need of rest, I needed shelter, and soon.

The Inn can't be far.

I expected the woodland to soon open up into a clearing. It frustrated me that only further trees lay ahead in my path. I thought of warmth, a glowing fire ablaze at my feet, killing the numbness of my toes. My stomach grumbled, forcing my mind to think about all the foods I couldn't consume.

It was then my ears suddenly pricked. My feet crunched along the snow, and I listened intently. It seemed a second pair of steps were following my own. With each step of mine, a second came from the rear, its sound replicating my own as the snow was compressed to the ground.

Spinning to surprise and confront my follower, I stood very much alone. The sound of steps stopped as I turned. Again, I walked on. And again, the crunching of snow came from behind me, this time the footsteps appearing much closer than before.

Again, I stood alone and paused, looking into the silent wood.

"Hello?" I queried. "Is anyone there?"

I glanced to the ground, only to see my tracks were the sole trail on the untouched snow. No second set of prints were visible.

I called out again. My only response, the branches of trees swaying overhead. All directions were deserted. Trees encircled me, and only darkness displayed past their strong stance. The noise appeared again. The crunching of footsteps started faintly, but soon its rate increased. Now the dashing of running feet trampled along the icy forest floor, but still no prints were present. Their sound appeared to get closer, and closer. I listened until the trampling halted dead in front of me.

Half expecting to be struck, I remained motionless against the tree's bark.

A slow, exhaled breath evaporated into the night air. I glared with astonishment, witnessing the cloud of moisture as it slowly faded into the atmosphere. The low sound of breathing lingered on in front of me.

But the struggling gasps for air were not my own.

I ran faster than I thought possible up the hill, at times grasping the ground to pull myself forward. Losing my footing, I slipped more than once, though I didn't stay down for long. I continued to stumble, intermittently looking back at my tracks.

With each rapid glance back, nothing appeared in sight. Still the footsteps continued to stomp heavily behind me. Tree after tree of the darkened forest I passed, my path never showing an end.

Regretting I hadn't stuck closer to the road was now nothing more than a torturous thought. While looking back, I tripped over a rooted branch that lay submerged beneath the frost. At that point, a clearing in the trees ahead appeared. A faint scent of smoke caught my senses as I rebounded from the ground, lifting my head and pushing myself up from the ice. I ran with my last ounce of energy.

Now the footsteps fell silent. Again, I constantly checked the land behind me, half expecting something to be at my heels. I struggled to maintain my sprint. Although the ground was slippery, I attempted to increase my speed, and for the last remaining yards, I crawled my way upwards to the clearing. Sighing relief to finally be out of the darkened wood I regained my stance.

I quickly dug my heel at the ground. The earth beneath the snow felt solid. I had finally made it to the road. The coldness sharply stung my eyes, forcing tears to run down my cheeks. Taking a brief observation of the area, I again froze. Set back off the road, on a small incline, stood The Dram Inn. The humble building looked more welcoming than I could ever have imagined. With my panicking state fading, I wandered upwards to the Inn, each step taking me closer to safety.

Chapter Twenty-Two

I approached the entrance. The Inn's door stood tightly shut. Before I gained the stamina to knock, a round-faced gentleman appeared through the narrow crack of the door. He held a plastic crate filled with empty bottles, that were then set gently down on the hidden step.

"You okay, son?" he asked, his voice high with concern and worry for the frozen figure he did not recognise. "Come, come, get yourself inside. You look like the breeze could knock you flat."

The gentleman himself was short and sprouted a thick head of ginger hair that parted to the far left of his crown. He appeared comical on first impression, but his caring generosity upstaged his amusing appearance. I thanked him as he guided me through to the bar area of the Inn.

Sitting me down at the corner stool, away from prying ears, he spoke softly. "What in God's name were you playing at walking about in such weather?"

Words formed around my tongue but struggled to progress further.

"Car trouble, was it, eh? Many folks believe they can take on the snow as they drive through these parts. Every one of them gets into a spot of trouble. Luckily for them and you, my doors stay open."

I nodded in agreement. "Thank you again."

He shrugged, suggesting no effort was made on his part. "Now, can I get you a drink? Perhaps something hot to warm your bones?"

I craved the thought before replying.

"Yes, please, a hot beverage would be extremely welcome."

My shaking eased steadily. The room's temperature was so pleasant that it forced my eyelids to involuntarily drop. My head slumped into my hands, and I leaned effortlessly against the bar counter. It was a voice from around the corner that caught my attention.

"If you want something to warm those bones, well, you'll have to throw back something a lot stronger than coffee in these parts." The voice was stern but, in some way, recognisable to me.

A glimmer from the fire shone on the opposite wall, and with it a shadow of a stiff figure repositioning itself from its seat, moving from the corner of the bar. The room unveiled more people present. At a quick glance, I counted five, no, maybe six people sitting in separate groups. They huddled together, all quietly seeking refuge from the storm. The fire was lively, keeping all the folk inside calm and comfy for now. In front of the flames sat two chairs. One was vacant, and on the other rested the figure of Mr Coull.

"Ah, Mr Wills, I had a slight inkling I'd run into your good self relatively soon. The word's about you're looking for me, hmm? What exactly could I be helping you with?"

The small crowd looked in my direction, intrigued, waiting for my response. Mr Coull leaned over the side of his armchair, he, too, patiently staring, awaiting my explanation.

"May I sit?" I asked in a somewhat whispering tone, hoping that the gathered guests would soon lose interest in my arrival.

"Of course you may, lad," Mr Coull shouted. "But if you sit with me, you drink with me." Whistling over to the landlord, he demanded my coffee be placed on hold and a tumbler glass brought to the table immediately. An opened bottle of scotch whisky was already keeping him company, its contents partly consumed by the man himself.

The landlord arrived over at the table and placed the glass down to pour me a double. He looked at Mr Coull with a slight cause for concern. "Now, Coull, I want a nice quiet evening, people are shaken enough. The last thing they want to listen to is you being sauced all evening." He directed a little smirk and wink in my direction, before Mr Coull summoned his response.

"Get yourself gone, Thomas. When have you known me to cause a bit of drama, eh?"

The landlord happily took the remark, giving the impression that this type of banter was part of their daily acquaintance. His exit from the conversation allowed Mr Coull to throw back his glass before placing it back empty on the table.

"Are you also here due to the storm, Mr Coull?" I asked only to break the silence.

Again, he poured another shot into his glass. "Nay, lad, I practically live here." He chuckled from his stomach. "Storm or not, lad, I guarantee you, I'd still be sitting in the same spot as I am now. It's nice to see the extra company around here, though. Usually it's just myself, and Thomas, the landlord, of course, who see the nights through."

The warm sensation of the fire on my frozen feet was exquisite, and as I took my first sip of whisky, my lungs came alive with heat, my wheezing breath completely subsiding.

"Are you a whisky drinker, Mr Wills?"

I grunted to the question, providing a temporary shrug in his direction.

"Have another, laddie." He tilted the bottle again, providing me with an overgenerous measure into the glass.

I leaned back contentedly, exhausted from the whole ordeal. Casually, I gazed amongst the clumps of guests. An elderly man, and what I could only guess to be his wife, sat beside an overfilled coat rack. A true impression of worry fell over the elderly woman's face as she huddled on her seat. All the while, the elderly man comforted her, embracing her with his arm tightly around her shoulders. He constantly whispered into her ear as she acknowledged with an agreeable nod. I had never seen the frail figures before, but there was something pleasant about watching them together.

A true image of love, perhaps.

Across the room were a family of three. A middle-aged couple, both possibly in their forties, sat at a table near the bar. They were accompanied by what I guessed to be their daughter, who lay soundly asleep, curled up against the corner of a booth. The couple didn't seem to interact with each other. The woman sat crossed-legged, contently reading her paperback book, and the average-built man sat, both feet resting on a barstool opposite her, staring into space. His pint of beer rested on the table next to him, untouched.

Comparing the couple, one wouldn't match them together. The woman was clean and well-kept, but the male seemed rough and uncared for. His clothes were baggy and tattered, his beard somewhat long and untrimmed.

The thought of siblings struck my mind. Although a band of gold encircled the finger of their left hands.

Nearer the bar, a woman sat alone, a glass of wine held to her chest as she continuously swayed herself slowly back and forth. Her face was half covered by lengthy jet-black hair and a silk scarf that wrapped tightly around her neck. There was a certain beauty to her appearance, but after viewing her from across the room, I felt sorry for her loneliness.

I glanced back at Mr Coull. He sat, glass in hand, staring into the flames.

"Do you know all these people?" I asked inquisitively.

He looked back at me, repositioning himself to get a better view of the Inn's guests. "Aye, I believe I do of sorts." He sat back around. "The old folk be Mr and Mrs Sullivan. They've lived in these parts as far back as my time goes. I even used to be good pals with Mr Sullivan's younger brother. That was back in my teenage years. Although, there's nae much to tell. Fell in love, they did, at a brisk young age. They never leave each other's side. Saying that, Mrs Sullivan has suffered with her health for some years now, barely remembers where she is. It's sad, but it's life."

Another whisky was thrown past his lips before he went on to his next target. "The younger couple behind me are the McCabes. Not had much to do with them myself. Although the gossip is, James McCabe works hard, breaking his back to the ground in order to keep his wife, Margaret, content. Nae a fitting couple, wouldn't you agree?"

I nodded, already thinking the exact same thought myself.

"She's from some city down south, Manchester maybe? Though I've never took it upon myself to ask."

"And what of the girl?" I asked with a flick of the head.

"The girl? Oh, that's their daughter, Bridget. Nice lass, pleasant enough. She moved up here with her mother, just before the couple married. Not many friends in these parts, though, tends to go off exploring the hills when the weather's fitting."

Again another drink was poured. But this time he offered me the bottle, to measure my own beverage.

"The woman sitting alone behind me, do you know her?"

Mr Coull stretched his neck over the side of his chair before promptly resting himself back. "That is Susan Daily, well-known daughter of Joe Daily. Her father's heritage was once an extremely respected name in these parts, and several towns over. He died some years back and owned a vast amount of land within the area. Automatically, Susan inherited it, immediately selling off what she could to provide for herself. She bides alone in a house next to Loch Borralan, keeping herself to herself. As many of us do."

I'd noticed that. I'd found it difficult to indulge with any local when trying to gather information of the man now sitting across from me.

"Now, lad, I believe that's everyone, apart from Thomas, who runs the Inn. Unfortunately, I can't tell you much. Tom's been here a good near on fifteen year. We tend to stick to being friendly acquaintances, nothin' more. The kind of relationship where he provides the drink and I just knock them back."

I briefly smiled at his comment, both of us staring back at the landlord behind the bar.

The time passed by quickly, our small talk never seeming to fade. The landlord handed out bowls of hot soup with an optional plate of buttered bread. The soup looked to be well received by everyone. Even the smell of it coming to boil made my mouth water. Later, I watched as each of the guests observed the progress of the storm outside, every one of them probably eager to return to their homes.

Gradually, as the hour grew later, they all settled for the night. The Sullivans were the first to drift off. Mr Sullivan restlessly held the hand of his wife, patiently waiting for her to doze before he attempted to get a good night's sleep himself. The McCabes were the next to slumber, showing no sign of affection to each other, burrowing under their blankets. Their daughter, Bridget, hadn't budged since my arrival, still lying peacefully on the corner booth.

Susan Daily remained awake for a little while longer, never indulging anyone with conversation. She sat quietly at her table, staring sharply at the storm outside.

As the time pressed on and the fire now fading, my mood altered. The last measures were poured from the whisky bottle and the glass slowly brought to my lips. The time was now to enquire on matters I couldn't explain.

Chapter Twenty-Three

The hour had now grown late, into the early hours of the morning, in fact. Every guest apart from myself and Mr Coull had settled into a sound sleep by now, including Thomas, the landlord, who vacated to the upper level of the Inn some time ago. Mr Coull sat watching the embers of the fire, his drunken eyelids attempting to slowly close. I was tired myself. However, I was in need of answers. And if I didn't ask now, I feared the time would never come.

"Mr Coull, we need to talk."

His eyes sprang open suddenly to my comment. "We have been talkin', lad. I'm sorry, but I'm well and truly exhausted, can this not wait until sunrise?" He spoke lazily, sinking his head further into the side cushion for comfort.

"It really can't. If I could provide a logical explanation, I'd indeed refrain from hassling you."

Mr Coull's head turned to face me, his eyes barely squinting through the dimly lit room. A sigh escaped his mouth. "You want to hear of the cottage on the hill. Is that right?"

I was astonished by his response. He knew exactly what I wanted to hear and seemed perfectly willing to suggest it. He leaned forward, combing his hair back with the palm of his hand.

"Okay. lad, but before I speak about matters that can disturb not only me but folks close by, please indulge me with what you believe to have occurred since your arrival at Elphin Cottage. And please, keep your voice down a notch. We don't want to upset any listeners."

And so, I did just that. I explained everything, allowing no detail, no matter how small to remain untold. I told Mr Coull of the first night I arrived. The ghostly tapping noises that appeared during the night, the unexplained unlocking of doors, and the emptiness of the mystery room.

I then spoke of the abandoned cottage that sat on the hill, its unexplained light source, and the sickly figure that stood at the edge of its boundaries, giving him as much description as I could provide. I described the figure's features, its white sunken face, its limbs of nothing more than skin and bone, and the clothing that hung loosely from around its flesh.

Mr Coull raised his hand. "Enough." His voice was stern and somewhat threatening towards my explanation. His hand was placed back to the arm of the chair, and his expression softened before he continued to speak. "Tell me of this evening. What in God's name encouraged you to venture into such risky conditions, and so poorly prepared at that?"

It was nothing more than pure panic that forced my leave. And after informing him of my frightening event, I believe I had justified my questionable actions to flee.

"So, you tell me. Am I going crazy?" I asked, now convinced that I would receive a comforting answer.

Mr Coull stared blankly at me through the dim light for the moment before leaning forward with a reply. "Nay, son, no, you're not crazy. Although if you mentioned this to anyone else, they'd likely convince you otherwise."

"Please, who is the figure by the cottage? And what does it have to do with Elphin cottage?"

My manner appeared more frustrated by the second.

"Calm yourself', lad, calm yourself'." Mr Coull let out a heavy breath, preparing to explain as discreetly as possible. "The folk you've seen are the Ferrell family. I can't explain why we see them, lad, we shouldn't. But every now and then, we see them all the same."

"Who are they?" I asked eagerly, intrigued by what I was about to be told.

"Shadows, lad. Just shadows of the past, nothin' more."

"You mean ghosts?" I enquired, my body lightly quivering.

Mr Coull looked up at me. A slight disapproving frown appeared on his face. "We tend not to call them such things, lad. But aye. You're quite right. Ghosts, I suppose."

I said nothing but patiently waited for the details to willingly fall from my storyteller's mouth.

"The Ferrell family lived on the top of that hill, within the ruin of the cottage you see today. Until death sadly struck them during the storm of eighteen forty-seven."

"Can you tell me what happened to them?" I asked, gobsmacked by what I was hearing.

"I can, lad. But it's no pretty story. In fact, it's a shameful tragedy to look back on. If you're eager to listen, then please, allow me to get it over with."

I nodded, intently listening to his every word as he brought back the shadows of the land's past.

Echoes of Home

Chapter Twenty-Four

Throwing back his glass, a full serving slid down with one fell swig. Coull hesitated, nervously pecking at the fabric of the fraying armchair, until the words eventually came to mind. "Alright then." He said, edging forward and beginning to talk.

"During eighteen forty-five, it was well documented that the land of Elphin were mainly known for its farming community. For many years, it was said the farmers who worked the land were content and joyful within their simple way of life. Managing to provide food and shelter for their loved ones was indeed their only priority.

"During the winter period of eighteen forty-five, the farming land was purchased by a new owner, and with this came a new set of problems. The person who now owned the lands was a man of wealth and nothing more. This very man already owned several impressive properties within the area, one of which was Elphin Cottage. His name was Peter Daily. He was considered a well-known gentleman of his time. And as I already explained, a very well thought of name within the nearest towns. To this day, it is a well-known fact that he had little time for his lower-class tenants, renting out his purchased lands to working farmers for the highest cost in the hope they would someday vacate from their homes.

"Daily would throw banquets for his rich and wealthy acquaintances on a regular occurrence, hoping to entice them to the beautiful lands of Elphin. Indeed, several higher-class families took it upon themselves to move to the surrounding cottages of the land. All the while, they looked to Daily as their advisor and friend.

"Elphin Cottage, known then as Elphin House, was newly built and located amongst the beauty of the landscape. A picture-perfect setting to anyone who happened to pass by. Though not all lodgings displayed such beauty.

"On the surrounding the hillsides and wastelands were countless stone huts. These were the dwellings of the farm tenants. Many of the lodgings that came with the land were in a desperate state of repair. Some structures showed no windows, and only a tiny door was access to its interior. With some lodges, the roofs had caved in completely, now with little or no shelter for its paying occupants. Many of the farmers protested their struggle to their new landlord, gathering together at the gates of Elphin Cottage. But Daily showed no interest in their plea. Not only were the dwellings disgraceful, but the land provided to them was poor. The lowest-paying tenant was expected to receive the smallest patch of land by

Daily. The land itself, boggy or rocky, completely unreliable for the working farmer to grow produce for the survival of his family. But still, Daily expected his extreme rents to be paid all the same.

"Times were getting harder for the farmers. But the worst times were still to come. Darkness would spread through the lands of Elphin in more ways than one."

I sat leaning forward, intently listening to Mr Coull's historical tale. He paused for a moment while the howl of the wind smashed aggressively against the entrance of the Inn. Pulling out a cigarette, he placed it into the corner of his mouth, then continued to tell his tale, striking a match and bringing it to his face.

"As the winter period of forty-five slowly came to a close, the farmers' spirits gradually heightened. Soon the harvest season of forty-six would be upon them, and with that came reassurance for all tenants. Food would be plentiful, and the demanding rent would be paid on time.

"Scattered rumours had set in many villages and towns nearby that, over in Ireland, famine had cursed their lands the previous year. The earth had turned bad, the people reported, leaving the population with diseased vegetation, unsuitable for human consumption. Of course, at that time, the desperation of Ireland caused no alarm to our Highland folks' way of life. Elphin had always been reliable for its harvest, and this year there was no exception. The crops sprouted healthy in appearance from the ground. As the days came closer, the merriment on the face of every tenant was proudly displayed. The communities sang into the late hours of the night, celebrating their good fortune and happiness.

"Then the harvest day itself arrived. It was always a special day. A day where all members of the family would help to gather crops from their rented plots. Husbands, wives, sons, and daughters, all eagerly willing to help out in the fields. Gayly digging up their grown produce, knowing that food would be available to them and their loved ones for many nights to come. Nothing was reported to have been wrong with the harvest.

"But several days later, Peter Daily returned to Elphin Cottage. It is said that as he was transported back into the lands of Elphin, he was awoken by weeping beyond his carriage door. Ordering for the carriage to immediately be brought to a halt, Daily listened to the weeping noises from his window. After only seconds, he was known to have vacated from his seat. He stood beside the road, gazing as if stunned at the sight of the surrounding fields. The farm grounds, as far as he could see were black. All harvest vegetation had rotted in the ground, that when pulled from its roots fell loosely apart in the tenant's hands. Like sludge.

"The smell of the harvest was sickening. Its rotting stench filled the summer air, and Daily quickly retreated to his carriage. And as the wheels continued to head down the dirt-track road, families could be seen sat huddled on the roadside. Their crying was heard in despair for miles, with no resolution for what they themselves were about to face.

"Despite the sight that Peter Daily had witnessed the previous day, he offered no generosity of any kind. It was time for rent to be paid, and he demanded his payment in full from his tenants. Days passed by. All the while, Daily remained at his cottage. Several of his tenants had called, pleading for help at his gate. Though not one penny was given by him in payment or relief to the tenants.

"It was on the seventh day Daily finally ventured out, accompanied by his guard to the dwellings of his tenants, not knowing what to expect. There was a written account from Daily's personal guard of what they experienced that day.

"Men, and women lay limp against the walls of their lodgings, sorting through the rotted food source that was now piled in a giant black heap. Children crawled on all fours sweeping the fields for anything remotely edible. Daily's guard himself stated he felt especially sorry for the children. The piercing sound of new-borns, screaming out in pain to their mothers in desperate want of food. Yet not an ounce could be given by their families. No emotion troubled Daily, and to the relief of the tenants, no payment was demanded during his visit.

"Daily returned home to write letters to the nearest towns in hopes that advice would be provided in kind. It wasn't long before responses came pouring back. To his surprise, similar circumstances had been reported as far as Inverness. The Highland soil had appeared to have turned sour.

"Time went by, but still no one could explain the reason for the vastly diseased crops. The rotting vegetation still covered the landscapes, and no farmer was seen tending to his plot in months. The people were starving to death. It took longer than expected for any relief to reach Elphin's lands. And for a short time, the people's spirits were uplifted. Coach after coach pulled in to their settlements, delivering Indian corn made available from the poor relief committees for collection. Still it wasn't enough. The food supplied fed only a third of the town's population, resulting in the remaining to seek relief in the nearest towns and the already weakened to slowly perish.

"As the men left for the nearest towns by foot, women walked back to their dwellings, their children in tears from the lack of food provided. Relief in the closest towns was just as short. Many men travelled twenty miles by foot each day to feed their families, only to be turned away at the door. Some men did not return home, too weak to make the repetitive journey. Their bodies would be seen dead on the roadside, covered in muck.

"It wasn't long before people completely lost hope with relief arriving at Elphin. So much so that the able-bodied lined up in their hundreds to attend the workhouses of Inverness. Although many tried, the poorhouse could not meet the demand of the needy. Many were turned away at the doors, the workhouse even struggling to supply food for its labouring workers. The meals provided were nowhere near nourishing enough for their survival. And with the odds of one working male needing to feed a house of six to eight persons, the poorhouse was relief that was doomed to fail.

"Soon, labour works were put into place. And for the people of Elphin, they would be expected to make the shorter journey to Ullapool for work. Several different labour projects took place, mainly the creation of roads by labourers, purely in exchange for food as payment. Skeletal men and women worked endless hours on-site, and many fell and died during the process of its making."

I interrupted his story, taking it upon myself to explain my visit to Ullapool only the previous day.

"Destitution Road?"

Coull paused, surprised at my statement, and nodded in agreement. "Aye, lad, that was one of the few roads built by the famine labourers. It stretches for more than one hundred and twenty miles and was created by the hands of those poor desperate folk. In fact, we use that very same road to this day. Well, only now the people call it something much different than Destitution Road."

Explaining how I knew of the road all made sense quickly to Mr Coull that he swiftly continued with his story.

"Well... While the labour works were in place at Ullapool, it was soon reported that Elphin had additional problems of its own. While some families were able to flee from the cursed lands, the people with no strength remained. Weeks had gone by. To anyone who passed through Elphin, the land would appear bleak in isolation.

"Peter Daily soon took it upon himself to investigate the farmlands for a second time.

Again, with the help of additional purchased aid. The following day, himself and several men marched into the abandoned farmlands. The once thriving village now appeared as a ghostly memory. The huts still lay in a state of ruin, the surrounding grounds dominated with mud. When each dwelling was investigated by Daily's men, it left them with horrific memories that would see them to their very last days.

"The first cottage door was tightly shut. Inside, the men found no fire lit but only two bodies curled up in a corner. Deathly figures of a man and woman, both human skeletons in appearance. On first impression, both were believed to be dead, but as the men drew closer, the woman screamed out in pain from her curled position, whimpering, desperately pleading for food. Her husband lay dead next to her, as he had done for some time. Not even she had the strength to move him.

"The next cottage housed no living but sickened the men who inspected the single room. No adult was in sight, though on the dirt ground lay four small lifeless bodies, believed to be around age six to eight, their emaciated faces contorted with pain. The bodies were covered in rags. The children had scavenged anything possible to cover themselves. Several other cottages remained abandoned. But on the fifth hut, the men found an elderly woman dead on a coverless bed. And what may have been her daughter sat beside her, both wasted to bone.

"It was a sickening day. A day that would not be forgotten by Daily or his men. The bodies were arranged to be moved from the huts and buried within a mass grave beside the village. As each of the unsightly corpses was carried out from the huts, rats ran in swarms into the wilderness, fleeing from the men's intrusion.

"Several of Daily's tenants, located on the outskirts of the land, were bleakly alive. Living in appalling conditions. They, too, a haunting resemblance to their deceased neighbours. The following day, arranged visits took place between Daily and his surviving tenants. For a show of humanity to his high-class acquaintances, Daily offered work in exchange for food and any necessary repairs to their damaged huts.

"Three of the residents refused his offer, stating that his pity for them was too late. The damage had already been done. Their loved ones were already lost from hunger.

"One family did accept Daily's offer that day. They were known as the Ferrells. Their shabby-looking cottage sat at the end of Mr Daily's private land and could be seen from the outer boundaries of Elphin Cottage. The family consisted of a mother, by the name of Martha Ferrell, and her two younger daughters, Mary and Sarah, their age only between five and six. Their father, Thomas Ferrell, had died during the making of roads that current year. Leaving his wife and children alone to survive.

"The family were given food paid in coin from Daily's pocket that day and, as promised, their cottage was repaired and retitled under the name as Clais Cottage, a title of Daily's choosing. The mother and daughters were given straining tasks, upkeeping the ground of Elphin Cottage where required. The two young girls were also included in the paid labour agreement. Every evening after tending to the property, they would return to Clais Cottage on the hill. Thankfully, they ate their one provided meal of the day.

"Over the months, the poor Ferrells went by Elphin Cottage, unnoticed to Daily. But still, they worked in all weather conditions, with only rags covering their backs to protect them from the cold.

"Soon, the old farming huts were torn down by Daily. He had regained his land, which he always wanted. The Ferrells watched from a distance as their old community was stripped from history. They could do nothing, now the sole survivors of the Elphin tenants. For months on end, the mother and daughters continued working for Daily, never once complaining, too frightened they would be thrown out from their home, forced to seek refuge in the labouring services.

"The workhouses were still operational but continually unable to cope with the high demand of the poor begging for relief. As the winter months drew closer, the upkeep of the grounds became less demanding. So much so, that the Ferrells' duties were halved, and in turn, their payment of food decreased by the day. It was an action thought justifiable by Daily. And despite their poorest of lifestyle, no further charitable acts were bestowed upon the already broken family.

"Soon it was noted that the children's appearance was viewed to be unsightly. A sight that Daily deemed unfit for such a beautiful location as Elphin Cottage. The children were soon confined to Clais Cottage under strict instruction never to leave. With no fire for warmth, no food for their bellies, they were to sit and wait, weakened, alone in darkness. All the while, their mother continued her endless labour in the grounds of Elphin Cottage without them.

"Over the Christmas period, Elphin Cottage was a place of glee for Mr Daily. It allowed him to exploit his wealth to his higher-class friends. Much socialising took place that brought high class acquaintances from farther lands. Much wine was consumed during this time, and his guests ate merrily during their stay. Impressed so much by his hospitality, many would lodge within the grounds of Elphin cottage for several days or more.

"It was good business for Peter Daily to make new contacts. He prided himself on being well known to others and the face of hospitality during their stay. Though there was still one who despised him. As an evening meal was brought to a close, Martha Ferrell looked inwards from the corner of the window. Daily's guests withdrew from the dining table, and Martha's cold fingers pressed against the droplet-covered glass. She gazed at the table. So much food had been wasted that evening. Food that would feed her children's crying needs. She thought of the delight on their faces if she was to return to Clais Cottage with meat and fruit on her person.

"The food would only be disposed of by her master, never once considering the position of his one tenant's misery, and the children kept hidden away from view. It was on that day that Martha took her chance. The guests withdrew to the living area of the house. This left Martha to go about the dining room unseen, clearing the wasted food for disposal, as instructed by Daily himself.

"The untouched food Martha separated wherever she could, hiding it at the rear of the house beneath the vastly piled linen. That night, she was undiscovered by her master for her theft. Martha walked briskly through the darkness to Clais Cottage, overjoyed to provide for her two young girls. She cared not once for the thought of Daily or the risk of being caught.

"Upon her arrival at Clais, Mary and Sarah lay shivering under a blanket, surrounded by blackness. Not even a fire comforted their poorly covered skin. On encouraging them to awaken, their mother presented the gathered food under dim candlelight, and for the first night in many, the girls sat happily, innocently eating foods that the wealthy took for granted."

Chapter Twenty-Five

Thomas, the landlord, skulked about the bar. His impression was of a man seeking interaction only on the bleakest of nights. Though, no matter where he wandered, conversation struggled to flow. No one would speak. No one but Coull. And as he continued to educate, his whispered words forced my jaw to uncontrollably tense and my fists to secretly clench beside me.

"The routine of scavenging became more of an occurrence than intended for Martha Ferrell. Yet, each night when possible, she would scurry through the house, bagging the wasted food left by Daily's evening functions. No one suspected a thing for some time. Not even Daily's servants saw doubt in Martha, nor did they have reason to. Although the discovery of her actions was inevitable. Martha Ferrell was soon caught leaving Elphin Cottage with a helping of fresh fruit from her master's table. That night, she was summoned to Daily to answer for her actions.

"Martha begged forgiveness, providing no justification for the reason of her theft, other than to feed her under-nourished children. However, Peter Daily's empathy had worn thin, and he declared he saw no reason for her notion and betrayal of his trust. That winter's night, the staff watched as Martha Ferrell was thrown from the house and escorted beyond the property gates.

"Martha screamed, pleading from those iron bars, hoping her words would some way reach the ears of her employer, though mercy could not be sought from Daily. He was a stern and cruel man to all his tenants, and Martha Ferrell was no exception.

"The light grew dimmer, the air colder. With all looking hopeless, Martha had no choice but to leave the gate front of Elphin Cottage and return home, back across the moor to Clais Cottage, where she would greet her girls in darkness, empty-handed."

I sat comfortably in my chair, listening with ease to Mr Coull's vast knowledge of the past. The words fluently flew from his mouth, giving one the strong impression he had relayed his story many times over. Still, it was surreal to think all these events had taken place where I now lodged. However, still nothing explained the happenings since my arrival.

Mr Coull paused momentarily.

"Then what happened?" I asked quickly.

Mr Coull slowly sighed, again pushing his hair back before making a response. "What happens next. Well, it just clutches my soul, lad."

He clenched his fist tightly toward his chest making the statement.

Although feeling sympathy towards his tale, I needed to hear everything. "Please, take your time," I whispered, giving him no encouragement to rush and the freedom to speak when ready.

He gave a swift nod and continued to talk.

"Now outcasts to their only reliable food source, the small family of three had nothing to their name and were soon threatened to be evicted from their home by Daily. Life had certainly never been bleaker for the Ferrells. Without working for food or a dwelling for shelter, they were destined for only one path. A path to which no parent should see their child venture.

"Days turned into weeks, and no communication was had between Daily and his past employee. On clearer days, Martha was seen standing by the riverside, collecting a pail of water. She would stand staring blankly at Elphin Cottage before returning home, her figure appearing frail and more weakened by the day. The children themselves had not been seen by anyone in months. But during the beginning of February, the staff of Elphin Cottage gathered at their gates and heartbreakingly watched Martha Ferrell dig at the ground beside Clais cottage, using nothing but her own two hands.

"The body of her eldest daughter, Mary, remained clutched tightly in her arms for some time after as Martha wept into the shoulder of her deceased daughter. Further crying could be heard by the staff, its source from Martha's youngest daughter. Sarah clung lifelessly to the doorframe, watching tearfully as her sister was placed gently into the muddy ground. The sight disturbed the staff greatly, many of them sobbed and glared at the struggling figures.

"Peter Daily received note that day of the death but offered no condolences regarding the reported events. Instead, he pursued the task of having Clais Cottage torn down to its foundations.

"As time went on, the coldness of February became present. Snow fell heavily across the land, providing a picture of beauty in appearance yet a mission of survival for the impoverished. People no longer ventured outside due to the weather's drastic conditions, leaving the few to seek the only refuge inside their darkened homes.

"It was on the 20th February eighteen forty-seven that a deadly storm masked the lands of Elphin, creating great panic and struggle for its inhabitants. The storm itself had started several days prior, but it was on the twentieth day that caused great concern for the people's survival. As the storm beat down on the lands that day, Peter Daily encouraged his fellow high-class neighbours to evacuate their homes and make the short journey through the deep snow to Elphin Cottage. There, he would keep them secure and rested until the bite of the storm had ceased.

"Indeed, all his neighbours were eager to take the word of Mr Daily, feeling they would be in safe hands and that no harm should befall them under his wing.

"The guests had arrived, and the servants were instructed by Daily to keep them as comfortable as possible during their stay. For a time, as the gathered crowd drank and ate their fill, the occasion seemed like nothing more than one of Mr Daily's regular evening events. And for a short time, the guests forgot their purpose there.

"As the light grew darker, the evening became colder. Although the fires of the house burnt brightly, the guest's concern showed. Anxiously, they watched from any vacant window, fear striking the face of each observer. Peter Daily persisted in comforting his guests, ensuring them that all would be well if they stayed under his care. All the while, he played host, never once considering the unfortunate souls of Clais Cottage."

Echoes of Home

Chapter Twenty-Six

"Martha and Sarah Ferrell sat alone, huddled inside the small darkened space of their cottage. Both had not eaten or seen sight of food in days. Scavenging had not been an option since the snow fell heavily, resulting in starvation for Martha and her already sickened daughter.

"They had already sold any possessions to their name for want of food. This left them to live with nothing more than an empty dwelling, a building which Martha knew only too well would soon serve them as a tomb.

"Young Sarah lay delirious with fever. Her mother grasped her tightly in her arms as they sat on the stone floor listening to the storm's rage outside. Soon, Sarah began to sleep restlessly, abruptly coughing, struggling for breath as she slept. Martha could do nothing but watch and wait, her daughter slowly deteriorating by the hour.

"The storm was at its most fierce, though all she could do was listen to the wind scream against the door of the cottage. She stood to her feet, departing from Sarah who remained on the floor, and watched her daughter's shallow breaths create clouds of moisture that sprayed softly across the cold floor.

"Rubbing at her arms for warmth, Martha peered out of the small broken window. All light from the sky had vanished, yet the ground reflected a beautiful white from the already fallen snow. Martha squinted, her sight just making out the lights and outline of Elphin Cottage. She had seen many people arriving earlier that day, many of them she had greeted while previously tending to the grounds of the house.

"She continued to observe Elphin through the gushes of snowfall. Sarah broke her mother's statue-like glare, coughing violently. Martha knelt, stroking her daughter's hair from her forehead, apologising under her breath for the life that had befallen them. Tears formed from the mother's eyes, rolling down both cheeks and soaking into her daughter's filthy rags below.

"How could life have treated them so shamefully, when all they needed was the simplest of means to survive? Yet, no matter what opportunity was presented, a life of punishment and hardship struck their path, pushing them ever further into the dirt of society.

"Martha looked about the four dampened walls that now sheltered only the two of them. Sitting, hesitating on her next decision, she peered across the valley. Regardless of whether she would again be thrown from the grounds or shown pity, Martha would take her daughter to Elphin Cottage in the hope to save her life."

My jaw rested open loosely. I hung on to his every word, disgusted by this Daily character he had described so vividly. What made his tale even more unpleasant was the direct descendant of Daily sleeping within such close proximity to us. Not that she was to blame for this story. After all, no one can pick their family, but the Daily name must have shadowed her for her entire life.

I looked over my shoulder. Susan Daily now lay still under her blanket, the only movement through the darkened room was the rise and fall of her steady breathing.

"The time of day was unclear to Martha, but the hour must have been late. Total darkness fell inside the cottage, as she touched the inner walls for guidance. She felt the tremble of her daughter's arm as she encouraged her to stand upon awaking. Sarah was weak. Far too weak to move. But she gained her stance and hooked on tightly to her mother's hips for balance.

"Martha knew the clothes they had would not keep them protected for long, they were hardly suitable for the warmer months. Both mother and daughter edged towards the door. The wind smashed against the wood's surface like a violent animal desperately seeking its prey. When the door was opened, the harsh weather pushed them back firmly, as if encouraging them to stay sheltered.

"Both figures stepped out into the snow. Bold footprints of panic trailed behind them that would soon be lost in time.

"The sky was solid black but still threw ice down from the heavens. The slope down from Clais Cottage was steep and slippery, as you yourself have witnessed. Neither mother or child had shoes to protect their feet. With each mistaken step, their soles and toes scraped with the sorest of cuts. Each and every step became more torturous than the last, until little Sarah could take no more. Losing her grip from her mother's waist, she hit the ground with a thud. The snow cushioned her fall, but now she remained still from exhaustion, her tiny body imprinted into the thick layer of snow.

"Martha paused, turning to view the remaining distance to Elphin. It hadn't altered much, but the lights of the cottage shone brighter through the driving snow. Although she hadn't the strength, she picked up her child. Sarah's face tucked into her mothers' neck, protecting her from the storm that attacked them.

"Once arriving on flatter land, Martha must have felt relief. A small bridge that led over the Ledmore river to Clais Cottage was still available back then, and a good thing, too. Martha scurried across the wooden planked bridge with Sarah still held tightly in her arms.

"The cottage was now so much more visible to her that she picked up her pace as best she could. Sarah coughed violently again into her mother's ear. Once she started coughing, she found it almost impossible to stop. Martha had tried many different herbal remedies throughout the months to fight the infectious retching fits, but nothing seemed to take hold of the problem or aid her symptoms.

"Soon, Martha stood at the metal gates of Elphin, her pulse quickening even faster than before. The sensation had her feeling faint and somewhat sickly inside. She couldn't turn back, not now. With daughter still in arms, she began her short incline to the home of Mr Daily."

Echoes of Home

Chapter Twenty-Seven

"The guests of Elphin Cottage had eaten their fill and now gathered quietly around the fire. Very little conversation was made as the guests' gazes panned over to each other, all of them waiting patiently for the first person to break into panic.

"Mr Daily kept the conversation flowing amongst them when possible, but no one had the desire to indulge him on particular topics.

"The silence soon broke when a female guest jerked up to her feet, screaming, holding out her pointed finger to the window. All guests looked in the direction of the woman's motion, all witnessing exactly the same image.

"A figure of more death than living stood outside glaring in at them from the frightening storm, the figure a ghastly sight of nothing more than skin and bone, its mouth almost toothless, its eyes sunken deep into its skull. The hair clung stiffly to its forehead, unable to move it due to the vulgar creature it carried.

"It took Daily but a moment to realise who again stood on his grounds, but the altered appearance sickened him further. 'Be gone.' Daily yelled with hate, embarrassed by what had come to his door. But the figure did not move, did not understand his hatred. It placed its cut and blistered hand on the glass, glaring at the folks inside.

"'Please… Help… Oh, please.' It sobbed, tapping its shaking hand on the glass. 'Oh, please, God help us. My daughter, she is extremely sick. She needs help, she needs warmth…and love, please.'

"The crowd inside gazed back at the weeping figure surrounded by snowfall, although not one budged from their place. The creature in its arms coughed aggressively again, the cold air tightening its chest all the more. The figure stroked her creature by the hand. And as she did so, a bloodied handprint on the glass remained.

"'Enough!' Daily yelled, his tone this time stern with anger. 'Be gone. There is no room for you here.'

"The figure continued to plead for aid regardless as tears fell from its sunken sockets, a look of desperation masked frantically on its saddened face. Many of the guests were appalled by such a figure. They placed their heads down to avoid such scenes, ignoring pitiful cries for help.

"'There's no room for you here.' Daily's voice thundered again through the living quarters and out into the creature's ears.

"'Take my daughter, just her, please?' it sobbed, now nothing more than a broken whisper through the glass.

"Again, no one budged or dared stare into its line of sight.

"'Please.' She whimpered. 'Don't you see her? Look at her. She's so cold, so tiny. Won't you look at what you will not assist?'

"Again, all heads remained motionless to the creature's call, and not one thought of sympathy was presented in its direction."

Chapter Twenty-Eight

A lump sturdily formed within my throat. A tearful gleam blotching my eyes, that I would soon blame on the warmth of spitting flames. Still, I said nothing. There was no need to speak. I was far too enticed by the end of his story to care.

"Martha placed her coughing daughter on the softly bedded snow, out of sight from the soulless demons within. She crawled her way through the ice to the main entrance of the cottage, slamming her palms recklessly against the sturdy wooden door. Again, no one came to her aid. No matter how much she screamed, cried, or pleaded, she went unnoticed by the huddled guests of the house.

"Soon enough, time took its toll. Martha jumped, noticing she had drifted to sleep for a moment. Yes, it had only been a moment, but she encouraged herself to remain awake. A light layer of snow had already blanketed her body from the waist down, and as she moved, the ice quickly crumbled into small piles by the sides of each leg, leaving a bodily outline on the steps.

"Her vision hazed, and she turned her head quickly to the daughter who remained in the same position her mother had left her only moments prior. But with no warmth, Martha returned immediately to her daughter's side. Sarah sat frozen against the stone wall, her coughing brought to sudden silence. Her head hunched over the top of her chest, allowing her knotted hair to conceal her purely innocent face.

"Martha embraced her daughter tightly, whispering sweet comforts into her frozen ears. It was then that Sarah's head fell limply to the side. The child's eyelids displayed open, though she stared directly through her mother. Her mouth slightly ajar, yet no breath filled or escaped her tiny lungs.

"Martha Ferrell screamed in grief and despair as her only remaining daughter now lay motionless, embedded in the snow. Weeping cries were heard from the house, a sound that seemed like more animal than human to the guests. Martha, too, sat against the stone wall, praying over her daughter's huddled corpse, rocking her uncontrollably in her tightened grip.

"She no longer attempted to gain access, to seek charity or humanity amongst these grounds. She, all her family and friends, had been dehumanized by the landowners and higher class of Elphin. They were no longer people, good people. People with families who loved one another, no longer children who played innocently and joyfully in the villages. They were looked at only as pests and vermin, an overpopulated nuisance to their society, that deserved the hell they'd been living.

"Martha's tears turned to icicles on her sunken cheeks. Holding back her screams of grief, she knew only too well that it would not benefit her in any form. Looking down at the child who appeared to be within the deepest of sleeps, Martha kissed her several times on the forehead, pushing her hair aside to display her beautiful face.

"The wind blew fierce, and the snow fell sharply, but for the first time, Martha felt no cold. She felt no pain. Quietly, she sat against the stone, staring out into the darkened distance. No worry struck her mind, and no desire to move was evident.

"The snow blanketed her body, yet all fear had escaped her as she again gazed down at her daughter. Martha soon slowly drifted off to sleep, a sleep from which she would never awaken."

This concluded Mr Coull's tale. However, I had so many more questions to ask, so many more details that must be known. He sat comfortably in his chair, his blanket now brought up and tightly tucked under his stubbled chin.

"So they were left to die? What happened to the bodies?"

"Oh… Well, the storm died drastically over the following few days, and all the guests quickly vacated Elphin, too disturbed to ever spend an evening at Daily's grounds again. The word is, that as they left Elphin Cottage, witnesses were greeted by two skeletal figures of a mother and daughter, both statues frozen in time from a night that is still remembered to this present day."

"And the bodies?" I asked promptly before he settled himself even more so.

"Nothing is really recorded, lad. However, they say they moved them back to Clais Cottage and were buried within the grounds. Two stone cairns are situated there, folks estimate this location to be the graves of the family. Now please, lad, let me sleep."

I didn't feel tired now, not one bit. His story had awakened me, leaving me intrigued to find out as much as I possibly could. His eyes shut as he again buried his head into the side of the chair.

"Is that who I've seen? Is it Martha Ferrell who stands across from the river? Who knocks and slams on my home?"

Coull's eyes remained closed. "All good questions for when the morning arrives. For now, I must rest, lad."

I relaxed back in my chair. The early hours of the morning chimes struck the Inn's clock, and as I closed my eyes to sleep, the heavy breathing of the local residents dominated the darkened room.

Chapter Twenty-Nine

The noise from the locals awoke me early the next morning. I had slept soundly throughout the remainder of the night, waking only once to manoeuvre myself from the stiff position of sleeping upright. The sparse gathering of guests hovered around a small circular table within the bar lounge, on which the landlord had supplied toast, cereals, and coffee on the house.

For any local who had money on their person, they were able to order something hot from the kitchen. The toast and coffee would have to suffice for now. Besides, at a glance, the small quantity of food appeared to remain untouched by any hands but my own.

Mr Coull ate no breakfast, but happily sat in his usual seat, a coffee in one hand and a cigarette in the other. Conversation was minimal as we sat, both still exhausted from the night's heavy drinking session. The landlord exited the room to inspect the outdoor conditions, reporting that the storm had calmed but the snow lay thick on the land.

"That's good enough for me," Mr Coull vocalised, providing the remaining locals with a surge of reassurance that it was safe to travel outdoors.

I stared amongst them. Worries that clouded their shadowed faces the previous evening had all but vanished, now leaving them all with a slightly pleasant glow as they sat mumbling amongst themselves.

Sighing, it wasn't long before Mr Coull got to his feet. "I'll be making my way, lad. Will you be joining me?"

Resting my half-filled mug on the table, my mouth still full with toast, I gave a swift nod, standing. Mr Coull smirked in my direction before beginning to make his exit.

The locals were right. I stepped outdoors, and the storm had indeed calmed, though the snow was amazingly deep in appearance. I took my first few steps, and its depth hit just below my knees. The air was crisp and refreshing, awakening my senses from their ever-so-drowsy state.

"What's the matter, lad? Letting a bit of wee snow keep you?" he said, not turning back. He continued to march on, clearing the wall of snow in his path.

I walked directly behind, making my trek less strenuous by using his trail to keep up. Coull ploughed through the snow, never showing signs of tiredness or annoyance. As I caught up, he trailed off from the side of the road and climbed over a small narrow gate. Looking back, the sight of The Dram Inn displayed somewhat different to how I'd imagined it in full light. It had somehow changed… And not at all to my liking.

"It's a steeper walk," he called out from afar, "but the trees shelter its path."

I soon followed suit, and sure enough, he was right. Soon, the snow came level to only our ankles, and as the way became steeper, even the path itself was visible. We trudged side by side up the woodland path. The birds sang infectiously, bringing the forest to life once more.

A complete reversed appearance of only the previous night,

"Do you know this path well?" I asked, trying to keep up with his stride.

"I know all the paths, lad, been walkin' them since I was a wee boy. Ain't come this way in some time mind you, the path has even started to grass over. It'll soon be gone and long forgotten."

"As everything always is," I replied.

He gave a short, grunt-like chuckle, nodding firmly in agreement. "Still, we must enjoy it while it lasts, Mr Wills."

As the woodland opened into a clearing, the path, which lead farther onto the hillside, narrowed and was at some points hardly visible as we strode. Still, Mr Coull knew these parts like the back of his hand, leaving me absolutely no need for concern.

Mr Coull's knowledge of the area astounded me. The more he spoke, the more I came to find his character likeable. His humour was quick and on point, a feature I found most surprising and unexpected coming from an isolated man of the wilderness.

Despite the tiring walk, our long discussion was pleasant, and his patience towards my queries never shortened. He spoke of having been a boy, growing up within the same lands. He spoke of little education but working the fields as his father had, and his father before him. He told me of the deaths amongst his family. His mother when he was ten, his father when Mr Coull was twenty-four, and his only brother at the age of twenty-eight, leaving him alone with only the land he had inherited. There was nothing more for him beyond this simple way of life. No excitement, no aspiration, no love. He seemed somewhat content regarding it all, so very proud of his homeland as he presented it to me while we walked.

The path soon dropped to a steep decline, weaving its way down to a snow-covered clearing that could be seen in the distance.

"Mind your step, lad, or you'll be landing flat on your arse."

"Better my arse than my neck," I shouted forward.

A burst of laughter was returned by the leading figure. I managed more than halfway, then slipped on solid ice that rested beneath the snow. It was when my breathing lowered from panic that Coull chuckled at my side.

"What did I tell you? Are you alright, lad?"

I nodded, shaking away the shock of falling.

"Almost at the bottom, just try and watch your footing."

The rest of the steep drop was more than manageable. In fact, I mimicked every step of the man in front, just to be sure. Once we finally reached the bottom, the land levelled to perfectly even. A small valley was in view, enclosed by hillsides that completely surrounded it, almost as if for protection. Amongst the land lay countless scattered rocks and boulders, some piles much higher than others. Coull swept the snow from one of the largest of rocks and sat himself down, staring shamefully across the valley.

"Where are we?" I enquired, confused, but looking in the same direction as my travel companion.

"This is the farmland I told you of last night, lad. Well, what's left of it."

He was correct. It took me a moment, but I could just make out the rectangular foundations that had sunk into the ground. The rest of the rubble was scattered throughout the valley, topped off with snow and frost.

The morning sun had peaked its way past the clouds, and by doing so, a steam-like mist rose from the jumbled stones.

"You say they were all buried here?" I asked, wanting a little confirmation from his story.

"Indeed. However, I can't provide the spot they were thrown into. I don't believe anyone has ever seen a record or researched these grounds."

I frowned, a little wary of his answer. "If that's the case, how on earth do you know it's true?"

Coull stood up from where he perched, slowly walking over to my side. "Because, laddie, folk never forget. Word of mouth has stood the test of time in these parts. Locals aren't willing to forget or dismiss such tragic events just because there's no' a piece of paper to hand."

He appeared somewhat annoyed at my challenge, so much so that he walked to the middle of the valley alone.

"I apologise," I called. "You disapprove of my remark?"

Coull stopped his slow footsteps, turning to face me again. "I never approve or disapprove of anything. Now, let's crack on, shall we?"

Not stopping to wait for a reply, he continued through the rocky area towards the other side of the valley, where two hillsides dropped steeply down, providing a narrow path leading out of the forgotten settlement. Before the confined gap between the hills turned a corner, I looked back at the wasted land, attempting to somehow imagine how it once had been.

The path itself was dark, letting in very little light, blocked by the hillsides' dominating walls. Several clumps of snow dropped from above, each time landing heavily on my shoulders, missing my head only by an inch.

"Not too far now, laddie," Coull called back.

I was glad of it. The walkway between the hills slowly opened up, and as it did, the faded path again turned to much thicker snow. Loch Cam sat below us in all its beauty, its beached edges frozen over to solid ice. We again walked along the hillside, careful not to lose our footing. A huddle of lifeless-looking trees sprouted from the earth, striking our path ahead. Mr Coull strode on through without effort. I followed suit but fell a few paces behind due to tiredness. When the branches finally cleared, a sight appeared before me that sent tingles up my spine. We had followed the back path to Clais Cottage.

Chapter Thirty

The cottage and its surroundings lay as silent as it had on my previous visit.

"You've been hereabouts before no doubt, Mr Wills?" Coull asked, placing his right hand on its stone wall for balance.

"I paid a brief visit." My remark was short, and I was somewhat cautious towards his question.

His hand remained on the wall for guidance as he slowly walked round towards the side of the building. The two stone cairns stood to its side, perfectly viewable from Elphin Cottage below. Mr Coull stopped in front of them, looking down on them with a heaviness in his heart.

"Never should have happened, lad, never."

I stood beside him, looking down at the pitiful pile of balanced rocks. A small stone the size of my palm lay half submerged beneath my feet. Giving it a brisk polish, I placed it at the top of the stack and bowed my head, stepping back.

"As they were frozen in life, they shall remain frozen in death," Coull whispered.

A prayer quotation I had not heard of myself, but I thought best not to question the remark.

We stepped away from the house, taking a small break by the rippling stream that ran down the hillside of Clais Cottage.

"Why do people still see her?" I asked, wiping the flakes of snow from my coat.

"Who?"

"You know who, Martha Ferrell."

Wasn't that obvious?

"Hmm, many people claim they see different things while passing through these parts. However, it may just be stories, Mr Wills… Just stories."

"Like what?" for some reason I knew he wanted me to ask.

"Well." He paused for a second. "If we were to be speaking of recent events, there was a gentleman who passed through on his way to visit his relatives at Lochinver. He drove through Elphin in torrential rain one evening and stopped abruptly when a figure caught the corner of his eye. He stated an ill woman stood on the roadside. When he jogged over to her aid, she wouldn't speak. She would not budge from her spot on the road. The gentleman then went to retrieve a coat for the lady, but on his return, she had vanished, gone from sight."

"And the man didn't report this?" I asked with surprise.

"Aye, of course he did. But the authorities have heard far too much of this natter. They believe them to be nothing more than Shellycoat tales."

"Shelly…what?" I spoke out.

"Oh… Nothing but myths, lad. A Shellycoat is… I suppose our equivalent of a bogeyman of sorts. It's known to haunt the rivers and streams of the Scottish lands."

"What for?" I asked with interest. "Does it wait to harm people?" I imagined a troll sitting under a bridge inspired by fable tales.

"No, they are said to be particularly harmless, although prone to trickery."

"I see." I never had any real interest in folklore, to me they were children's stories. Tales with a grimness only to set fear into the young generation's minds. I wanted to get back on to the subject at hand. "Any more events that spring to mind?"

He waited, then shook his finger into the air, reminding himself of another incident. "Then, this time last year we had a couple of hikers, young couple they were. They burst into the Elphin café one morning, all panting and excited, claiming that something was following them in the woodland. They said they didn't see anything but heard footsteps of someone all around them. Shook themselves up pretty well before reaching the café, so they did. I just happened to be there eating breakfast when they stormed through the doors."

I said nothing but reflected on my own experience during my trek to The Dram Inn.

He took a moment, considering what next to share. "Ah…let's not forget the last owner of Elphin Cottage before you."

My ears pricked up as though called to attention.

"Can't remember the chap's name. However, there seemed to be no point learning it. I haven't known anyone stay there too long, but this man was here little less than a week."

Neither of us spoke for a moment as we watched the snow intermittently fall from the branches to the pulse of the breeze. And although the stream was not completely visible, its water could be heard clearly, flowing briskly against the rocky banks.

"I wonder what caused him to leave so quickly," I pondered the thought out loud.

"Indeed, lad, that is the question. However, I expect he experienced something of a similar nature to yourself. Some folk spook easier than others."

Mr Coull remained comfortably sitting on a sheltered rock. I stood to my feet, taking another look back at the abandoned cottage.

"Did anyone meet this man?"

"No… I myself only glanced at him from afar, but come to think of it, he did leave some belongings scattered about the place after vacating. Myself and a few locals took it upon ourselves to box up what was necessary, placing them securely inside the storage shed. Nothing that took our interest, of course, just bits of files and papers."

I had visited the shed multiple times, never once noticing a secure box of papers. "So, you just trespassed into his home?"

Mr Coull returned a glare of annoyance back towards me. Maybe I'd overstepped the mark.

"Hardly trespassing, lad. The man had gone, leaving the door to his home swinging upon its hinges. After several days, there was no sign of the anyone returning, so we took it upon ourselves to close up the house."

His glare softened as he stood, and without a word, he descended the hillside. I watched him quickly disappear between the thick bushes before following behind, very careful to not slip.

We reached the road by roughly midday, and although the snow still lay thick, there was a short sense of warmth shimmering in the air. The road was still closed to vehicles, but walking became less strenuous, and we quickened our pace over the covered road.

Slowly, the chimney of Elphin Cottage peaked into view, and as we reached its gates, its presence provided me with a sinking feeling that swirled deep within my gut.

"Would you like me to see you settled, Mr Wills?"

I hesitated with a response, and although my appearance probably displayed a form of cowardliness, I nodded in return.

Everything remained as it was left. The car completely covered in snow, the shed doors completely thrown from place, presenting the right door clinging desperately to its frame. The door to Elphin gently swaying from side to side as we approached. I was far from eager to set foot back inside, although nothing seemed to faze Mr Coull. He stepped in and made his way down the corridor to the living area, almost as if it were his own property.

"All seems sound, lad," he muttered, appearing to investigate every nook and cranny.

I had personally checked each room myself, a routine that now was getting far too frequent for my liking. The coast was again clear, though I expected nothing less. It wasn't until I returned to the lower floor that the kitchen displayed a surprising shock. Food lay scattered across the floor, scraps half chewed, and in some places, only the shredding of the packaging remained. Whatever pots and pans were placed neatly in the cupboards had been thrown from place, shattering the floor tiles on impact.

Mr Coull approached from behind, sighing as he, too, now discovered the scene.

"What the hell?" I shouted. "Who would do this?" I turned to Mr Coull for some form of support.

"Not who, lad, what. That door's been open all night, son. It'll only attract animals looking for food and shelter. Without a doubt, they've scurried in here with the intentions of finding food, and that's exactly what they found."

"What kind of animal would do this?" I spoke in some form of disbelief to his opinion.

"Wild cats maybe? Although we don't see them as often as we used to. Judging by the tears of this wrapping, I'd be guessing a creature with claws."

"I've never heard of them. Not in this country anyway." I brushed his comments aside as local rubbish.

"You'll spot them at night, lad, especially as they dart across the roadsides." He chuckled.

Regardless of this conclusion, I had lost all my food stock, leaving me with very little at all until conditions bettered. I knelt, clearing the filth-covered floor, throwing everything that may have been touched by a creature to waste.

"Tell you what, lad, my place isn't too far. I have a spare room, why not spend the night with myself?"

I pondered on the thought. Although I had come to like Mr Coull, I still didn't know much about him. The very thought of me lodging at his home seemed to bring on a sense of unease.

"I've plenty of food, and I'm sure it will prove to be more to your liking than a house with no power and nothing to eat." He grinned.

He indeed had a point. The company alone would be far more appreciated than spending the evening alone. I agreed to his offer with thanks, continuing to clear up the mess.

"Very well, lad." He patted my shoulder firmly. "Get what you need. The weather's still not cleared, and with this snow it'll take us an hour or so to reach home. I'd rather make haste and get there before dusk, if that's to your liking?"

Chapter Thirty-One

By the time we reached Mr Coull's home, the light had already faded. His house sat nestled between two rocky hillsides, just over a mile from Elphin Cottage. The surrounding lands were occupied by sheep that stood hardly visible, camouflaged by the vastly settled snow.

The house itself was more impressive than I'd come to expect. Its large structure seemed to almost dominate and climb up the rocky mountain wall's surface at either side. I stepped inside, and the house provided an instant warmth. Two large dogs came bounding around the corner, leaping to their master, happy to see him from their night spent apart. With all the excitement, both dogs hadn't noticed my presence as I stood several steps behind their owner. It took only a moment before both caught sight of me and fiercely growled.

"They won't harm you, just not used to strangers is all." He had to shout over the continuous snarling, holding both dogs back by their collars as they yelped, saliva spraying past their sharp white fangs.

I slipped past both mutts and into the first room, displaying a pleasant though somewhat hesitant smile. Shortly after, the dogs were let out to have run of the land, and Mr Coull returned, shaking the dog fur from his tattered trousers.

"Rascals, they are, yet wouldn't hurt a hair on your head."

I doubt that very much. I thought, though smiled and sat comfortably as I waited for my host to join me.

We ate and drank our fill that evening, and despite my awkwardness at staying, I felt the most content I'd been in such a long time. The dogs were let back in the house, and regardless of my worry, they showed no aggression towards me again. One of them sat beside me as I drank, resting his head on my thigh as I gently stroked his ear.

I looked about. Photos hung on the wall, Mr Coull's relatives, some not even known to Mr Coull himself, yet he explained he kept them hung up out of respect for his parents.

To awaken our senses, we decided to catch a breath of fresh air. As we stepped onto the wooden porch, an external light flickered an unusual yellow, brightening up the darkened area.

The cold was bitter but still refreshing. And in a sense, I found it more than a comfort to know that warmth was at my demand.

I placed my hands in my pockets and a piece of card caught my grip. Pulling it out, I lifted its contents, slowly toward the light of the lamp.

"Of course, how could I forget," I muttered. I had spent so much time with Coull over the past night, yet somehow, I managed to forget all about the one answer I was originally seeking.

The photo itself was more creased than previously but still displayed a clear image of the aged gentleman sitting in front of me.

"Where did you get this?" he asked, gazing down at an image he had not seen in many years.

"Amongst the clutter of the cottage. More importantly, why was it taken?"

By the lines on his face, I could tell he wasn't too impressed by my questioning.

"What makes you think it's of any importance? It's a picture, is all." His reply was stubborn and somewhat sharp.

"Well, the man, who is he? And why was the photo taken?" I asked wearily, not sure whether my questioning would bring Mr Coull distress.

He keenly handed back the photograph and continued to smoke unceasingly, the cigarette never once leaving the slight gap in his mouth.

"Nothing to tell, lad." He spoke in a patronising tone. "Due to the reputation of the house and lands, a memorial was put in place, donated by yours truly. The other man you see is a local historian." He paused, puzzling his mind for a name he had perhaps long since forgotten. "John… No, Jim Tariff was the man from what I recall. I never really got to know him. He showed a keen interest in the land's past, then one day he just left. No one's seen him since. Mind you, he was somewhat older than myself. He's probably near to passing by now.

"The inscription on the plate, can you translate it?" I enquired, passing the photo and the written piece of paper I had stored in my pocket back into Mr Coull's hands.

He looked at the image hard, squinting both eyes narrowly at the sheets. "It's somewhat blurred, lad. However, I remember what it says.

The location and the date you now know of. The bottom reads in Gaelic. *Le ùine thoir mathanas don pheacadh again."* He spoke the words fluent and clear.

"What does it mean?" I asked with a build-up of anxiety pounding deep inside my chest.

He casually handed the papers back with heavy sorrowful eyes. "In time, forgive our sin."

Echoes of Home

Chapter Thirty-Two

The next morning, I awoke early. So early, in fact, that no one seemed to stir on account of my departure. A scruffy, handwritten note had been left for me by the door, explaining that Mr Coull had gone out before sunrise to circuit his land, and if I were to leave before his return, he would pop in on Elphin Cottage to check on my well-being from time to time.

Not wishing to overstay my welcome further, I prepared for the short yet strenuous walk home.

The morning was indeed fresh, and as I looked up at Mr Coull's house, frost had surrounded its exterior walls, almost glistening, the sun shining down on the surface of the aged brickwork.

I saw no one on my return home. Only the sound of crunched snow beneath my feet was to be my company.

I took my exit from Mr Coull's land and paced myself to make it back to the cottage with good speed.

By the time I reached the entrance to Elphin Cottage, my chest had tightened, in turn causing a faint wheeze with each and every breath. On appearance, Clais Cottage sat peacefully in the distance, surrounded by a blanket of white.

A much prettier image than my previous memory.

I turned towards the upwards path. Surprisingly, the house inside remained untouched, and as I rested in front of the unlit fire, I couldn't help but reminisce on the strange occurrences that had happened over the past few days.

Would things now settle? I pondered, now the anniversary of such bleak times was at an end. Or would the sights and sounds of the unnatural continue to torment the innocent of this house, that did nothing more than merely sit across from its land? It was a question I could not answer. But without doubt, I was only bound to find out.

I sat and rested, regaining my strength, trying desperately not to fall into a deep sleep. Instead, I picked a book from the shelf and skimmed through its contents. It was an old book, its title *Agnes Grey* by one Acton Bell. The author was not known to me at all, but I had never had a mind for literature. I also failed the imagination and attention to finish any novel that was put to my hand, regardless of who had rated it.

I began the very first chapter, and my interest gave out in little less than a minute before I skimmed the pages once again. The aged paper was tinted yellow at the edges, and as I flicked through the page numbers, the crinkled paper wafted a strong scent of dampness that had embedded itself into the contents of the book over many, many years.

It got me curious to wonder who the last person was to indulge themselves with these tattered pages and whether or not that person found the author's words meaningful and satisfying of their committed time.

I closed the book, tapping on the leather-bound cover with my palm. I paused for a moment, then quickly turned to its title page. The publishing date was the year of eighteen forty-seven, a horrible year for Elphin. But what alarmed me further was a neatly handwritten note, situated on the left-hand corner of the page, its writing preserved as clearly as the day it was written. And as I peered down over the dated handwriting, my shoulders became tense, my breathing shallow.

Dear Mr Daily.

I write to you with some happiness. It has been six months passing since my husband and I left Elphin, to which we feel no regret in doing so. The memories of your land shall be forever imprisoned in my thoughts and nightmares, regardless of however I wish them to dissolve.

Nonetheless, I wish to show my gratitude towards your care during that month of February. Without doubt, it was a worrying time for all. But without further doubt, it made us all feel a little less human by its end.

I wish you and your future all the very best, Mr Daily. And I hope over time Elphin may recover from the bleakest of times.

I would reassuringly like to wish you a merry Christmas, and I hope you enjoy this small gift. I remember your fondness for literature.

Yours sincerely,
Mrs A Jefferies
22nd December 1847

I glanced hard over the dates for a final time before the book was again closed firmly shut and placed on the table. The book itself was owned by the only man who had contributed so much misery to others, so much suffering. And although the man himself had long since passed, his belongings – this book – had remained on a dust-ridden shelf for all these years, never once moving from its spot.

What else belonged to this man?

Could it have been the very chair I sat in was his? The bed in which I slept, or bath in which I lay?

It wasn't worth justifying such thoughts further. I decided to instead search the storage shed, in hunt for the papers of the previous occupier Mr Coull mentioned. The shed's doors hung wretchedly from their hinges and now swayed loosely at an angle, scraping the icy floor.

Inside, there were many boxes filled with endless papers, the majority of them meant nothing to me at all. I spent several hours on my knees searching and was about to give up when I came across a file filled with written papers.

Again, these papers seemed of some great age. And what shocked me most was it was none other than the handwriting of Mr Daily himself that lay spread on each page.

Now sitting more comfortably on a bundle of cloth, I wrapped the collar of my coat tightly around my neck to keep in the warmth and flicked through the papers to my dates of interest, then began to read.

Echoes of Home

Chapter Thirty -Three

18ᵗʰ February 1847

A storm is brewing. I can now feel it in my bones. Many of my friends have now begun preparations. They have no idea how badly this storm will hit us. I shall allow them to continue their calmed plans for now, but soon I feel I must intervene. My only hope is that they shall listen to caution.

19ᵗʰ February 1847

It has already begun. The snow has started to endlessly fall from the sky, stopping all operations in its path. The majority of my staff have ceased working, to that I have ordered them to take shelter where possible. Many looked displeased by the matter, but that is no concern of mine. The rest of the staff will continue to work in the house.

I have given urgent instruction to my housekeeper, Mrs Donald, to make haste and call upon my neighbours, advising them to travel to Elphin House as soon as humanly possible. They are best to seek refuge with myself during such unpredictable times. The worst is still to come, I know it. Yet, they are safest here, under my watch alone.

20th February 1847

The parties began to arrive in the early morning, many of them by foot. They certainly made it in good time, too. Now the snow really begins to thicken. I have greeted them with reassurance for now, leaving them in the caring hands of Mrs Donald while I finish reading any remaining correspondence. It is only ten-thirty a.m. Hopefully more have received word and arrive promptly.

I am pleased to write, my house has been well-received. It is now five-thirty, and the weather outside is at its worst. I have instructed the staff to keep our company as comfortable as possible. They dare not complain of such a request. They, too, fear being thrown out into the cold. Such feeble creatures they truly are. They protest for each other, yet as soon as one is threatened, they fall under the heel of my boot without question.

It has now been days since a peep has been whispered from their lips in regards to Clais Cottage. Especially in my presence. The parasite

*who crossed me shall soon get what is deserved.
That is if they still live. The staff believe me to
ignore such pitiful pests. But I keep my wits about
their movements. The cottage was due to be
demolished days prior, though no company would
make the journey in such conditions, no matter
how much currency I offered.*

*Hopefully, the storm shall bring it to its
foundations soon enough. For now, I cannot think
about such feeble complications. I must play host
to the people who truly matter.*

22nd February 1847

*It was sympathy I caught in every individual's
eyes. At first, I mistook it as nothing more than
fear that burned through their souls. Now I see
that my first conclusion was so much further from
the truth than I so strongly expected. The
following day, no one spoke. In fact, it seems as
though many avoided my reassuring gaze inclined
in their direction.*

*The snow ceased yesterday, but far too hazardous
was the land for my guests to return to where they
craved the most. The day had passed by fast
enough, although many sat in awkward silence,
waiting impatiently for the clock hands to pass the
hours.*

This morning the weather was bleak, yet I felt it

safe for the people of Elphin to return to their comfortable homes with the aid of my staff. As the doors of the property opened, the gasp of every man and woman was heard clearly from my halls. It was a sight that no respectable citizen should have to witness, yet they did all the same. My, how some of them wept. I believe I will remember their sorrowful whimpers as they walked off my land until the day I die. It was then I knew they felt only sympathy for the deceased and nothing more.

Yet one thing troubles me the most. Would my peers always think less of me?

I witnessed the bodies myself during the early afternoon. A child, curled up on her mother's lap as they lay huddled beneath the window. The snow that surrounded them already beginning to melt, displaying wasted arms and legs, their skin as white as the snow itself.

I removed myself for a short time, instructing my house staff to move the frozen bodies from view. They have been placed in the back room of the house. Not an ideal situation by any means. But it will suffice until further snow clears and graves can be dug. The room itself has always been unoccupied, so I see no reason for this to cause disturbance. The staff will tightly wrap the bodies in layers of sheets, hopefully to delay any smell drifting out and through the house. For now, all I can do is wait until the workers arrive. I will be nothing but glad once this nasty business is concluded.

24th February 1847

Both bodies were taken from the house this morning, thrown onto a cart to be transported to the burial site. The small church itself is too far a distance for the workers to venture, so I have requested they be buried on the land of Clais Cottage. They didn't look too keenly on the idea, with no priest present. However, they were soon persuaded with a little extra coin for their troubles.

They finally departed around midday, and although the ground will be difficult enough to penetrate, a shallow grave will have to do. As for Clais Cottage, it is no longer of concern to me. The land is of no use at present, and I'm sure over time the cottage walls will slowly crumble to the ground.

26th February 1847

My house staff are beginning to try my patience. They silently putter about the property, whispering of recent events. They will no longer go near the room where I instructed the bodies to be kept. Several of them claim to have heard movement from within. It is preposterous. The room is nothing more than empty. And regardless of my explaining the obvious, they continue to disrupt the house with their constant gossip. Mrs Donald has escorted some staff to the burial site, supposedly laying wildflowers upon the three graves. A rather pointless gesture in my opinion, but hopefully their superstitious nonsense will soon come to pass.

27th February 1847

A terrible dream struck me last night. I know it was nothing more than a dream, but it felt so real. It has turned my health rather sideways. So much so, I have been unable to lose the bitter chill. All day the fires burn bright throughout the house, yet I still shake continuously under my woollen blankets. It has been a trying week. Maybe bed rest is exactly what I need.

1st March 1847

I have been bound to my bedroom quarters since Saturday. This sickness has hit me like a shot to the flesh. I write this entry while upright in bed. And regardless of my rest, the disturbance of dreams continues to persist. The staff are driving me to insanity. Many of them will no longer venture in close proximity to me, in fear of catching an illness. And it was only this morning that Mrs Donald reported two of my servant maids have now vacated the property. Apparently, they can no longer stand the unexplained noises of the house. In doing so, they have left their job behind them.

I shall not accept them back inside these walls. Not as long as I draw breath. The cook continues to feed me, but I have no appetite for his dishes at present. For now, all I can stomach is soup. I shall stay here in bed until this has run its course.

3rd March 1847

I hear more of my staff have left my employment. Now only Mrs Donald and the cook still remain a part of the household staff. I have offered Mrs Donald a raise in her wages, if not only a reassurance to myself that she will not consider departing from my company. Absolute fools, the lot of them. How dare they just leave. I only wish I could regain the strength to leave this bed and confront them all. Have they no pride? No respect for themselves? I think not.

It appears I have received no visitors since the ordeal. Not so much as a letter has been brought to my attention. Could it be that everyone wishes to wash their hands of me? Or perhaps more time is needed to overcome such distressing events.

Blast this cold! Must I remain in bed for an eternity? My body is still dominated by the chill. My sleep is disturbed with horrific thoughts. When will this end?

5th March 1847

Absolutely preposterous! No one came to my

service this morning. I resulted in anger by banging on the floor like some wild brute. I finally ventured out of my room and down to the lower levels of the house, only to find it completely deserted.

They have all gone… All of them.

The master now appears to have become the servant. I am forced to prepare my own food and dressing attire! I will soon hire on new staff. They are easy to come by. I just need a day or two to gain my bearings.

6th March 1847

Have I gone completely mad? I write this entry now, not knowing if what I place on paper is actual truth or purely imagination. Have I become so unsettled that I can no longer tell the difference between dream and reality? Perhaps reading the account back to myself will cause my nerves to see reason. Or worse, the defined truth.

Last night, after locking up the house, I lay in bed, unsettled. I must admit I am not that used to the house so deserted. The quietness of the rooms seems to disturb me some, having been rather used to the hustle and bustle of the past staff.

I believe my eyes finally began to drift when a noise from below caught my attention. At first, I believed it to be nothing more than Mrs Donald returning from her unexplained absence. But after calling aloud more times than one could count, I decided to venture downstairs. Luckily, a candle was already at my disposal, and as I ventured farther downwards, the noise appeared to become more aggravated by my presence.

The doors remained firmly locked, yet a constant breeze circled the house. I wandered the hall, until walking past a room that displayed the noise at its loudest. It was indeed the room in which the two bodies were kept. I am tired, you must understand, with such utter nonsense. I felt absolutely no hesitancy when I turned the handle and entered the room. The noise stopped in an instant. I held the candlelight higher to project its beam, and it came as no surprise to see the room lay bare. It was then that I noticed the candlelight's image on the blackened window. And to that matter, the person who held it. For it was not I who held the light, but the reflection of Martha Ferrell's sickened face that stared back at me.

Echoes of Home

Chapter Thirty-Four

My hands shook uncontrollably as I read Daily's personal accounts. So much so that I placed the papers down, wondering whether to continue reading at all. Only a couple of pages remained within the crumpled stack, which were likely to be his only documented account of the matter.

I looked around surreptitiously, as though expecting figures to linger beside each shoulder. I was alone, no one stood in sight. The afternoon's light was not at its strongest, so I decided to move, sitting on the bench at the front of the house.

Turning the page again with much anticipation and caution in order to refrain from causing further damage to the documents, I peered at the final two entries. The final words I would ever read of Peter Daily.

8th March 1847

The noises appeared again last night, yet I dare not sum up the courage to confirm what I had previously witnessed. The room shall now be kept under lock and key. The window itself, I have barricaded with materials available to hand. No one should set foot in there until such insanity ends. I have managed to spend the morning out of bed, but soon I feel the tiredness sweeping back into my body. I may rest a little while more. It has been a productive morning.

It's happening again. Right at this particular moment, while I write with trembling hands. The noise calls to me when the land is at its darkest, insisting to eagerly gain a reaction from my persistent stubbornness. I shall not give it the satisfaction. I shall not go down there, not to face that...that thing again.

Why will it not stop? The mantel clock has just struck three. Still, the sound continues to rattle through the house. My patience can no longer tolerate such mockery. At a time, I contemplated facing the demon that tormented my mental state so, but while leaping from my bedside, I caught a glare of light that filtered faintly through the curtain. Crawling across the floor space like vermin so as not to be detected, I peeked through the narrow gap of material. What I saw in the distance, in full light, was Clais.

9th March 1847

I am leaving. If only for a short time. Having relatives and a property located at Oban, it seems only fitting for me to visit now of all times. These past few weeks have been mindfully exhausting, but I'm sure the change in atmosphere will be most beneficial to me. I dare say it will give me time to add some additional poetry to my works. I may even take the short ferry over to Lismore for a time. The nature there is quite marvellous from what I recall as a child.

As I waited for the carriage this morning, the house seemed so isolated. It felt as though I was in fact viewing its interior rooms for the very first time. The carriage arrived shortly after midday. A stocky man dressed in rather ragged black attire saw to my baggage while I comforted myself on the seat cushions. Peering through the carriage door, I took one more look over the house before calling out to the driver. As the wheels began in motion, the view of the house swung out of sight in seconds.

I have come to understand, this is not a goodbye to Elphin. More than likely my return should see me back during the summer months. Yet, as the carriage jolted over the cobbled entrance, I felt as though I should never look upon this land with the same light again.

The driver made the swift turning to join the road whilst I looked out of the window. Clais stands in the distance, darkened by its past. A past that I myself willingly encouraged to forge at my own will. As we moved farther from view, I poked my head out of the window for one final look, Clais's stature now becoming smaller by the second. Its structure could even be mistaken for any other dwelling but a ruin. But as the sound of the horse's hooves echoed from the ground and the driver's tuneless whistle pierced irritatingly through the spring air, I continued to gaze on with a frightful stare. I saw two girls playing around crumpled walls. And a motionless woman standing above a freshly dug grave. Her eyes never left me, until the cart turns from sight.

Echoes of Home

Chapter Thirty-Five

Placing the papers beside my lap, I thought hard with regards to the words written in faded black ink. On one hand, it presented an element of truth to Mr Coull's historical facts. On the other hand, it gave no concluding evidence to what Peter Daily, or I for that matter, had actually seen on several occasions.

Could the hidden truth really be that the disturbing presence of the Ferrells still continue to linger through the land? And after all this time, too. Daily's writing did, however, explain the cause of the barricaded room inside the house, the window obviously boarded in a panic, and the emptiness of its space. What I couldn't quite put my finger on, was why the papers that shook to my side were so easy to possess. Surely, they belonged in the possession of the village's local archives. Yet here they were, stored away carelessly inside a damaged wooden box.

Whatever the case, they were now found. Wherever they had come from mattered little to me.

The papers were not placed back in the box but carefully refolded and gently inserted into the inner pocket of my jacket.

I'm sure someone would find them of interest.

After a little short of an hour, I had managed to examine the remaining content of the wooden storage containers, finding nothing more than dampened books, rusted jewellery, and piles upon piles of unorganised billing receipts. I decided to cease searching for any further evidence of the previous owner.

What would it mean to me finding a name anyhow? Nothing.

Upon restacking the boxes, I happened to notice a large torch that stood slanted against the wall of the shed. It was doubtful such an item would still function, but to my surprise, it powered up instantly. After closing up the shed to the best of my ability, I managed to get the car running. It still sat peacefully surrounded by a white wall of snow.

As the engine warmed, I stood beside the car for a moment, mesmerised, watching how the breeze patterned Loch Cam's wide surface. Such scenes still gave the location a hint of magic for me. And it was scenes such as this that would stay with me forever.

It was pushing on to late afternoon. Resting on the chesterfield, I thought anxiously of the evening ahead, no longer wishing to play the victim to such occurrences. After much indecisiveness, I decided I would take matters into my own hands. No longer would I hide, run, or scare, all whilst sitting within the house, scurried away like an animal trapped in a cage. Tonight, I would discover my bravery. Tonight, I would face the unknown. Tonight, I deemed myself worthy of resolving the mystery.

*

As the evening drew to dusk, I remained slumped in my chair, nervously awaiting the fall of daylight. I could find nothing better to do with my time but wait. And waiting, without doubt, seemed like the best course of action to me at this particular time.

Looking into the mirror, I saw a scruffy image portrayed back by my reflection. I'd go as far as to say the man staring back at me could almost pass as a Highlander himself. If he continued to remain unshaven, that was. I possessed no razors to improve my look but managed to tidy up my appearance by trimming the untamed hair with a pair of rusted scissors found beneath the bathroom sink.

The eyes that once looked fresh and sharp now presented a strong, squinted feature. And below displayed two dark patches that clung desperately underneath both eyelids, an evident sign that rest had not come easy since my arrival to Elphin. Still, I rinsed my face with cold water, the sensation shocking my senses instantly, that now in turn sharpened my restless mind.

What time is it?

I couldn't tell, but as I dried my face roughly on the cloth, the toll of the clock struck from below me.

Echoes of Home

Chapter Thirty-Six

Mr Coull sat comfortably at his kitchen table. A cigarette stub taken from his mouth was forcefully smothered into an old tin tray that had not been emptied in some time. As he let go, ash fell from the sides of the container, leaving an unpleasant grey smudge on the table. He patted about his body confusedly, until a new box was found inside his chest pocket. He smoked again, the cigarette never once leaving his mouth until the next would be lit.

The day had not been an exhausting one, yet he was at an age where it no longer took much for his bones to ache and for tiredness to cloud his mind. He sat back, groaning, placing his palm on the stiffness of his lower back.

"Damn thing. To Hell with it." He cursed, continuing to massage the aching muscles.

The sight and smell of his smokes lingered in the kitchen. So much so that his dogs no longer showed their presence in the same room. To anyone else, the dryness of the air would cause sudden breathing difficulty, but not to him. He had become immune to the stench and the thick wall of smoke that clouded the rooms, staining the wallpaper to a colour of an unpleasant piss yellow.

He awoke earlier than usual that morning and, believe it or not, it was the urge to smoke that broke his sleep. After readying himself, he quickly made his way to the porch to let out both his excited mutts, slipping past his living area.

Leslie Wills lay dead to the world, snoring from the comfort of the sofa. He'd come to think fondly of the lad. Out of everyone, he himself knew only too well of loneliness, living alone for more than thirty years. It was now more than second nature to remove himself from others. Mr Wills would soon understand that. But for now, he would watch over him.

He dared say he saw a little of himself in the lad from the time they had spent together. There was a particular air of trust that Coull felt for the young man. A trust that did not come by often. Due to the events that had occurred over the past few days, young Leslie eagerly took in each and every word of his knowledge with interest, and more so respect. This was something Coull had not encountered often in his lifetime and probably why he'd taken such a shine to the sleeping figure in his house.

Let the boy rest.

He slid on his boots. After scribbling a note that would be found easily enough by Leslie, Mr Coull walked onto the wooden porch, closing the door as gently as possible behind him. The dogs bellowed over each other with a keenness to lead the way, always stopping at a distance to ensure their master followed casually from behind.

The morning had not yet hit first light. However, Mr Coull knew his way regardless. Despite his restricted view, he arrived at the border of this land and made a sudden turn that shortly led him to the only narrow road that cut through Elphin. It was a steep downhill walk from here, but at its peak, it offered marvellous views in whatever direction one looked.

Coull walked in the centre of the path, having no concern for oncoming vehicles or black ice while trudging downwards through the melting snow, knowing only too well no vehicle would dare venture on this route. It was far too risky.

He followed the curve in the road, and several cottages came into view, though it was still too early for lights to show from inside each dwelling. In the space of an hour, the light would rise, and folks would be going about their business, seeing to their daily duties as usual.

He walked past each tiny house, visualising how they once looked when he was a child. These structures had been about long before he was born, and they would stand long after he had passed.

The café was next, some three hundred yards farther down the bank. Coull thought about this old building most of all. It had once served as a school for the tiny populated area of Elphin, but that was a time when more children were local to its area, some many years ago from what he could recall. When the school closed its doors for the final time, the remaining parents had no choice but to journey their child to Assynt, although that school also closed many years ago.

As his feet crunched past the old school that now read Elphin Café, good memories flowed through his mind of his teachers and friends, all of which were no longer a part of this short life. Even though the building had changed some, Coull could still picture himself and his friends at play, chasing each other around the old stone building, as both his parents once had before him. If only he could turn back the clock. How he would love to see his old friends just one last time.

Both dogs had now lost their stamina for leadership and appeared more than content to return to their owner's side. Giving both mutts a little sign of appreciation, he patted his knee twice before continuing to walk.

"Almost there, boys, almost there," he calls, encouraging both dogs to again pick up the pace and walk steadily in his company.

By the time Coull finally came near to the bottom of the hill, the sky was slowly showing its first glimpse of morning light.

"Just in time. We can't see much in this light, can we?" he said, though only to himself.

A little farther on, a small wooden gate painted black came into view, that if one was to drive on past, you would barely realise it existed. The gate was not locked but opened only when much force was applied to its rusted hinges. A small dirt path ran between countless birch trees that covered the narrowed walkway's edges at either side. The path was not long but a little muddy. The trees had covered the path from the storm. Now water from the melted ice seeped continuously into the dirt channel.

Both dogs again went ahead, marking as many trees as they could find. Soon the path ended, opening up onto a small patch of land. A dry wall surrounded its borders, the piled stones covered in thick spreading moss. When the season was at its warmest, the small clump of land displayed the most vibrant green grass you would ever see. Though now, only snow spread deeply over the surface of the ground and, coming up from beneath, the greyness of aged headstones.

Coull didn't look around. No one visited the site anymore. He himself had tended to the one acre of land for the past twenty-seven years, and for the past ten he'd never crossed paths with a visitor, even if one stumbled on the grounds accidentally.

The far-left side, nearest the dry wall, marked the reason for his visit. Walking steadily enough through the grounds, in order to not misplace his footing on any of the smaller monuments that had been engulfed by ice, Mr Coull made his way to the far side of the graveyard, occasionally looking back, making sure his dogs had not strayed back up the path from where they came.

To the right of the walls stood a building that was once used for religious purposes. It was incredibly small and long since out of use. Nothing now filled its interior other than a small selection of Mr Coull's land tools, although he tried to maintain part of the building as best he could.

It had survived since its creation in the early seventeenth century and deserved as much respect as could be given. He paused, stopping in front of a stone that towered above the ground and angled slightly to the left. Snow capped the top of the stone's edges, though he left it undisturbed.

Coull said nothing for a time, only gazing on the faded words that had been chiselled into the stone's surface years ago. He still held great love and affection for the people who lay there. And whether it was pure emotion deep within, or the coldness of the morning air, a single tear rolled briskly onto the whiskers of his unkempt beard.

He wouldn't stay for much longer. Both dogs, although sitting, continued to whine impatiently for their master to make haste from his spot. Giving one final pause before retracing his steps, he called his dogs to attention.

"Won't give me a minute, will y'all?" he projected, both mutts playfully scratching at his thighs, panting excitedly at his return.

He walked to the entrance of the path, and another headstone caught his eye. This was much different in appearance to the other withered stones in the yard, and even more so as the ground nestled around its heavily cracked base had been allowed to wildly overgrow.

The headstone was large, and what one could imagine as having been tremendously expensive for its time. Yet it sat in the darkest corner of the graveyard, left to be forgotten. A darkened moss dominated the majority of the surface, though in sections its lettering appeared perfectly clear. Without any further need to inspect it closely,

Coull frowned walking past the sight, as he always had done before, reading only the first two lines of the engraving.

At Rest
P.Daily of Elphin House

He swiftly returned his attention back to the narrow path, slowly walking towards the painted gate. By the time he arrived home, Leslie Wills appeared to have left without note. The day's conditions were in fact the best they had been in a number of days, and as Mr Coull slumped back into his chair, the dogs duplicated the action of their master by collapsing to the wooden boards, too exhausted from the morning's venture. A cigarette was taken from behind his ear. He smoked it quickly, as usual, thinking of his young friend and the troubles he had encountered.

Chapter Thirty-Seven

I stood leaning against the front gate. Since the daylight had faded from the sky, I thought it best to vacate the house, not wanting to experience similar events as a few nights prior. Elphin Cottage was fully alight behind me, a land marker should the torch fail upon my return.

"Come on," I whispered with anticipation, my eyes never leaving the ruined cottage of Clais fading in the distance.

The time was not yet late, though I preferred to leave at the earliest convenience. Regardless of my eagerness, I remained outside for what felt to be hours, but still nothing out of the ordinary occurred. Daydreaming for a time, I thought of the person who'd made this venture possible. I wondered what had happened to my brother and if he in fact was aware of the unfortunate situation of the area before gifting me with a troubled chunk of its past.

How was he to know?

I shrugged off the idea with a shudder.

A group of Highland deer casually grazed on the nearest hillside. A picturesque scene, despite the poor evening light. It was a sight I thought would always be taken for granted in this part of the world.

The last of the daylight quickly drained from the skies, leaving me surrounded with eerie silence. Not even the sinister sight of a dull moon shone through the clustered clouds.

I thought the time dedicated to standing here was nothing more than wasted, but as I tiredly hung against the rusting metal bars, my head tilted to the sky, a dim light faintly glowed on the hill.

For a time, I only observed the swinging light of the lantern. It occurred to me that although the air was peacefully still, the lantern swung frantically through the darkness, almost as though Clais Cottage was dealing with a storm of its own. The flame of the light shone a dazzling white in colour, and I squinted intermittently at the blinding object, then shut both eyes in protest.

Clenching the flashlight tightly in my hand, I slowed my breathing and lifted the hood of my jacket. Slowly, I retraced my steps to Clais.

The journey would hopefully not be as tiring as my first attempt. I had taken a clear mental note of the path Mr Coull led us on only yesterday. This path, of course, dismissed the barefoot crossing of Ledmore river and avoided such a risky inclined trek in harsh, icy conditions. Yes, the snow still lay inches deep, but I felt I was becoming a better judge of the land beneath my feet than when I first arrived at Elphin. And a better judgment meant caution and care. However, I'm sure many would refer to my horrendous walk in the moonlight as foolish and unnecessary, regardless of the situation.

"It serves the poor bugger right," they would say if anything at all was to happen to me. "Got no one to blame but himself."

Maybe it is foolish of me?

But by the time I reached the old bridge, I had managed to dismiss all of my reasoned doubts, crossing with care, remembering the old planks caused an aggressive slip if trodden on with haste.

My flat feet slid carefully to the other side of the bridge. With my sight now becoming more accustomed to the darkness, navigating the winding path appeared to be far more manageable than I'd expected. The small trees that sprouted nakedly from the hillside continually aided my climb up the rocky path.

I took a brisk look back. Elphin Cottage still remained in full light and reminded me of the distance I had already travelled on this strangest of nights. I rested for a short while, giving time for both legs to ease from the throbbing sensation that took my breath away.

The land about me remained so deafeningly quiet. Much quieter than before. I stood and listened intently. The atmosphere appeared hauntingly surreal as the only noise that trembled through my frost-bitten ears was that of my own heavy breathing.

Chapter Thirty-Eight

Coull jolted upright from the comfort of his chair. He looked about the darkened room, fumbling for the light switch, placing a hand on his chest to steady himself. He exhaled slowly as though into a paper bag to calm himself. It was a thought that had broken his relaxed state. And now that he was back within the real world, he could no longer recall what panicked him.

Worry circled around his aged body, a sickly feeling that swung frantically about his stomach, and he momentarily heaved, bending over his shaking knees. He sat back, wiping the beads of sweat that fell from his temple. Both dogs did not stir. They were now so used to their master's coughing episodes.

"Don't get up, ma wee boys." Coull spoke sarcastically, holding his hand outwards to where each dog lay.

A single eye opened from their curled position, that again shut tightly as they continued to sleep.

The thought of worry did not stray far. He sat for a time, trying desperately to remember the dream that awoke him with fright. He couldn't recall the last time he had dreamt of anything. Although he found it typical that now he had, he could remember nothing either way. The sickening feeling soon diminished, though the worry that clouded his mind did not rest. It continued to jump from pillar to post. Something certainly didn't feel at all right within him. He thought of his new friend before coughing violently into his hands, soon almost gasping for breath as the cough which he had become so accustomed to, took hold of his body, disabling him to the spot.

He pulled his hand away. Red dots lay smeared across his palm, a sight he'd seen before and now caused him no further alarm. He wiped the redness from his hands and stumbled to his feet. Breathing as steadily as possible, Coull swung a coat around his shoulders and left the house, the door slamming aggressively behind him.

Chapter Thirty-Nine

I clambered upwards through the trees, my pace slightly quickened. A full moon suddenly burst through the wall of darkened clouds, throwing a pale light down amongst the steep landscape.

Not much further.

I reassured myself of the questionable venture I had taken on. The torch that was still grasped tightly in my hands was now put to use, shining the way forward through the cluster of branches. It wasn't much longer until I realised that I had somehow managed to lose the path entirely. While concentrating on ducking the many branches, I must have somehow gone off course.

No matter.

I knew if I continued in the current direction, the house on the hill would be unmissable. It was overly typical that the power of the torch should die when it did. I stood isolated in the bleakness of the withered woodland, frantically smacking the side of the torch in desperate attempt to revive its brightness. It was then, as I looked farther up hill, that I spotted an even brighter light that shone through the branches, its swinging intermittently pausing its sharp beam.

The torch dropped to the ground behind me as I climbed to the blinding light source. I only now began to wonder what I would do once I reached the top. To be truthful, I wasn't quite sure, though the closer my destination appeared, the more desperate I became to find out its secret.

As I pushed aside the final two branches, Clais Cottage came into full view. The lantern continued to sway vigorously, and the inside of the cottage appeared to remain completely untouched by any light. I stamped through the tall grass to the front of its door, and again, I froze. The air remained so still, yet the lantern swung as it always had.

"How? How is that possible?" I said, regardless of who may have heard.

I reached out to settle its swing, and the lantern suddenly ceased its frantic movement, and at an unnatural angle, as though time itself had come to a complete halt. Its light now shone even brighter, frozen in position. I worked up the courage to reach out for the lantern's handle once again, and an unsettling noise of faint whimpering flew out from the glassless front windows.

Whimpers of sadness, desperation, fear, and loss. These were all feelings that sprang to mind as I listened intently to the continuous moans. The door already sat ajar from its never bolted position. Leaning forward, I peered with one eye through the line of its gap. I could see nothing inside, yet the sorrowful cries could be heard without struggle. I had stood inside the walls of this cottage before and even viewed with my own two eyes its ruined interior, its crumpled walls, broken roof, and the dirt covered floor. I knew the noises were not of any living thing, but of a past that would never allow itself to be forgotten.

Hesitating, I withdrew my steps. The thought of retreating down the side of the mountain as fast as humanly possible suddenly came to mind. But it was the voices of the past that kept me in place. They were echoes of home. And regardless of my fear, the cries wished for me to hear them; to help them.

I would not run, not tonight.

I stepped inside, and a gust of energy swirled around me, a feeling I could not explain further or, for that matter, ever feel again. The whimpering continued, though projected, bouncing from each wall, providing me with no direction of the source.

Dizziness instantly clouded my mind, my lungs feeling several times lighter than usual. Each breath felt endless as my chest never seemed to have its fill of air. The sobs swirled around the room, never once stopping due to my presence. Slouched against the wall, my sight hazy, I shouted over the buzzing noises that were forced into my ears.

"Let me help. I'm here to help."

Yet the noises did not stop. And covering my ears did not stop the now torturous sound from reaching into my mind. The surge of energy pushed me to the dirt on the floor. I could no longer recognise if I were breathing at all. My chest seemed paralysed with fear. Yet the beat of my own heart pulsed rapidly about my brain.

Holding out my hand as if to protest against the torture, I spoke as loudly as I could manage. "Please, stop this… I don't wish to harm… I don't wish to hurt. Who are you? TELL ME WHO YOU ARE!"

The sound heightened further, and I could no longer bear its torment. I fell to the floor. My face lay smeared in the dirt and scattered animal filth, my senses now utterly lost, leaving me without the realisation of knowing if I was still a part of this world or within the most disturbing of dreams.

My body was pressed tightly to the floor by a force; a force that unbelievably could not be seen. Any more and I should surely burst. I tilted my head to the side with extreme struggle and whispered words through the buzzing that prevented me from hearing any other mortal sound.

"Please, give me the name of your loved one who was so wronged in life… I shall see them right."

Although the energy continued to press me farther into the dirt, the noise abruptly silenced. I again heard my heavy-paced breathing, the ruffling of soil beneath me as I struggled on its surface. A noise of movement came from the corner to where my head reluctantly faced. It took a moment for me to identify what I saw. The faint outline of a child appeared engulfed by darkness. No facial features were identified. Not even clothing hung from its outline. The child remained still in the lightless corner, only tilting its head to the side where I lay.

"Please… Tell me." The words fell from my mouth before falling into blackness.

The child's outline did not move. But faintly, a voice slowly presented itself and spoke in the most innocent of tones.

"Martha was her name."

The child I gazed at seemed to float back into the darkened corner from which it came, until it was no more. Words could no longer escape from me to call the child to my aid. Exhausted, my face fell to the dirt, and blackness followed.

Echoes of Home

Chapter Forty

I awoke unaware, not knowing if I had been out for minutes or hours. Mud lay smeared on the side of my cheek, and as I pulled myself upright from my stiffened position, I casually wiped the filth with the sleeve of my jacket and sat back against the cold stone wall.

I waited for the sensation of shock to pass and my breathing to steadily return to a much more normal pace. For reasons I could not explain, the memory of Kate's smile drifted in and out of my troubled mind. The recollection of her beautiful lips, intimately moving only for me, as they did all those years ago. Yet, no memory of her voice. *Had I forgotten this already?* The picture of her replayed over and over. Until finally, the fixation broke.

I looked about me, not wanting to remain in such a place any longer than necessary. The gloomy space now appeared as nothing more than innocent. The energy that before controlled my body, now had evaporated from my senses. Even the deafening noise that almost broke my mind had vanished. And again, all I heard was the swinging of the lantern outdoors.

Though something still did not feel right.

The outline of the child who'd spoken to me from the corner had completely faded, yet the sensation of watchful eyes glaring at me continued to cause concern for my safety.

I looked again at the corner. Still now, only darkness covered the area. I wanted, no, needed to leave promptly.

I pulled myself up to my feet, my legs unsteadily dropping beneath me. Again, I tried to stand, using the protruding rocks of the wall to aid my stance. Both legs shook tremendously, almost as though they were no longer under my control to command. Still, with both hands on the lightless wall, I guided myself to the other side of the room and through the doorway, never once looking back.

I fell, the thickness of the snow cushioning my fall. For a short time, I didn't move. The snow, although cold, felt somewhat comforting. It was a feeling I had never ultimately considered before, but it helped to calm my state of shock. My throat, as dry as it was from dust, struggled desperately to swallow only the night's air.

Picking up a clump of snow in one hand, I took several bites from my palm, relieving my throat in an instant. My head bowed, I took a brief moment to myself before having to retrace my steps down the hill.

Come on. If you don't move now, you won't move at all.

Sighing, I briskly shook my head in order to regain my bearings. It was then that the lantern glowed its brightest, swinging frantically as though it would at any second tear itself from the bracket embedded in stone, and cast shadows in motion around where I sat.

Again, it elicited a sudden panic within me, and I jolted upright, taking several steps back in order to avoid whatever the cottage would be about to reveal.

The lantern's swing slowly calmed, though my trance did not break from its sight. It was then a sharp breeze brushed across my face, flowing over the cottage itself, and in my direction. I glanced down, watching the cooling air ripple against my dirt-covered clothes, before I gradually turned to face the direction from where it blew.

I instantly narrowed my eyes to the distant view of home, bearing witness to the dark figure that stood lifelessly at the door of Elphin Cottage. It was as seen before, motionless, yet the brightness of the house lit up her features more so than previously. I listened carefully, not knowing whether to believe my own sanity. Faintly, through the valley, the tapping noise I'd come to know so well, travelled through the breeze.

"Martha?" I said, only to myself, questioning the figure's presence.

Nothing was whispered, there was only movement. The skeletal shadow of what once was, turned her head towards Clais Cottage. The gaunt, terrified eyes of Martha Ferrell never once blinked but pierced straight through to my soul. It felt as though for an eternity she didn't move, only glaring back at the person who stood at the door of her past home.

A lump formed deep in my throat as pure terror impaled me to the spot. The image of Martha again turned towards the brightness of Elphin Cottage, yet no footprints remained from where she had stood. With the slow motion of her weak wrist, she rapped on the glass of the small cottage window. In my frightened state, I could only watch her. Watch and observe, hoping that if I studied the ghost-like figure for long enough, the mystery of her living existence may unfold. However, it did not.

Due to the coldness of the bitter night air, a welling of tears polluted my sight. It was as I quickly wiped the tears from my chilled face that another figure came into view. This figure, I was glad to admit, did not appear ghostly in the slightest. Its walk presented as far too quick, striking its feet through the uneven snow, leaving a tunnel-like trail in its path.

At first it was near impossible to identify the walking figure, as shadows of the road near masked its presence. It was when the figure marched towards the entrance of Elphin Cottage that the identity of the wanderer was revealed. The light of the house now faintly outlined the stranger as it grew closer to the bright, solid structure.

Mr Coull walked with a certain eagerness that caused me to think he may have been walking with panic. He hadn't reached the cottage, though the gates were soon upon him. And now I felt only determination to warn him of what he would face once his quickened tread came to its end. I called out, my voice desperately attempting to travel its way across the lands and to the ears of my friend.

Mr Coull's stride did not stop, or slow for that matter. He continued to plough his feet through the ice, each step taking him inexorably nearer to the cottage. I tried again, and again, though my attempts were deemed failures at reaching Coull's attention in time. If only he were to look to the ground. He'd evidently notice a trail of my own, clearly visible from when I left the grounds earlier that evening. Instead, he kept his head held high, looking towards the lights of the cottage.

All efforts to shout now appeared useless. The wind suddenly increased, and any call was lost the moment it was projected. All I could do was stare as the aged gentleman finally reached Elphin Cottage.

Coull stopped suddenly, bearing witness to the image of Martha Ferrell who now stood directly outside the cottage door. Coull spoke. Of what, I could not hear. But his gravelled voice seemed to somehow reach where I stood. He edged closer, holding out his palm, indicating calmness. Martha immediately ceased her motion and gradually turned to face her caller. He stumbled, falling backwards in the snow at the sight of Martha's glare. Caught in a trance his head did not turn away from the spirit. In fact, his glare seemed magnetised by her as he fell.

Yelling to Coull out of instinct, again I realised it was still no use. I needed a distraction. But what? Waving my arms frantically certainly wouldn't cut it, I knew that much.

I looked about me, my sight landing on the swinging lantern. Both Coull and the spirit remained in intense eye contact.

If I used the lantern to grab Martha's attention, Coull could make a run for it.

Certainly not the most cunning of plans. It was nothing more than a simple trick of misdirection. But all I needed was a few seconds at most. It had to work.

I ran up towards the light, snatching the lantern. The bracket fell loosely from its bolted place in the crumbling wall. I swung the white light in a manic state, so hopeful to gain the attention of Martha and aid Coull to safety. I waved the heavy metal with both arms, praying that it would somehow catch the sunken eyes of my target. I held the light up to its highest and caught sight of the woman moving her head curiously in my direction.

"Run… Run, you fool," I said through tightly clenched teeth.

Yet Mr Coull did not run, did not move, his sight fixated on the location of Martha, his hand still held outright in her direction.

"Come on, get out of there now," I shouted.

This time, a flinch of a reaction was made by Coull.

Had he heard me?

I called again, so hard that my voice broke on screeching my final words. Martha still looked toward me, saddened yet intrigued. And it was at that moment Coull, too, turned his head and stared hesitantly in the direction of the floating light on the hill.

Success broke my concentration. A brief smile spread across my face as I peered over to my friend, still lying huddled above the mounted snow.

Blackness immediately followed. The light that shone so brightly from the windows of Elphin Cottage had dispersed, engulfing the house and land across from me in perfect darkness. Coull could no longer be seen, giving the impression he had been wiped clean from this world. The wind had dropped its strength dramatically, giving me the urge to call out for my fallen friend once more. Only no voice answered. Neither did the light return.

Chapter Forty-One

I ran as fast as humanly possible, forgetting my weakened legs, striding down the icy hillside. The lantern, still held tightly in my firm grip, aided my way with its shining beam, assuring me I'd again find the path from which I came.

Soon, I found myself through the cluster of entangled branches that grabbed and clawed viciously at my skin, then out onto the solid ground of the narrow path.

Now for the tricky part.

I braced my feet down the steep dirt slope, and avoiding any lethal dips that suddenly came into view demanded skill in this light. More so as I constantly scouted the distance between my steps. Elphin Cottage remained only a patch of darkness in front of me, a worrying sign that the same appearance would address me upon my return.

Stumbling only once, impressed I had caused no lasting harm, I reached the bottom of the hill and sprinted in panic, forgetting almost instantly the ice-covered bridge ahead. It was a close call, as both feet immediately lost their footing, almost sending me tumbling into the freezing water that now quickly flowed beneath its planks.

I fell against the riverbank, hitting my shoulder with a violent thud on impact, landing on nothing more than scattered stones and beached wood. I moaned, my jaw tightly clenched shut in order to embrace the sharp stabbing pains that jolted through my side.

"Idiot," I called, the pain influencing my statement further.

The fall had abruptly knocked the wind from my lungs, bringing on an unpleasant heave, consuming my breath. My chest felt ablaze with fire while I attempted to suck in each short breath my body would allow.

I sluggishly staggered towards the path, my pace for a time much slower than before, although the lantern was still surprisingly in hand. I brought it up towards my opposite side, pressing against it tightly for support.

Despite my eagerness, it took just short of an hour before I reached the roadside. It was far more time than I'd expected, persuading me to think that only the worst had come to Mr Coull.

With the road black ahead, it was still easy to lose my bearings in my current state. And if I didn't pay close attention, I would miss the entrance to Elphin Cottage entirely.

I almost misjudged the turning. The clang of the large iron gate startled me as it gently rattled on the side of the solid stone pillar.

Thank God.

My weakened steps took me through the entrance of the property. The sight in front of me was bleak and quiet. If you weren't to know, you'd hardly expect there to be lodgings there at all.

The sound of footsteps filled the air. Loose ice and gravel crunched unwillingly beneath my feet, openly alarming anyone of my unwanted presence.

I never once knew exactly what I expected to find. The driveway turned its corner, now displaying the unsettling look of the shadowed cottage.

I looked to the ground. An uneven patch of snow lay moulded where Coull had fallen, yet no indication or trail followed what had happened to my friend shortly after. Surveying the grounds where I stood provided me with nothing more than uncertainty. Knees down to the ground, I inspected the fallen shape in the snow.

"Coull? Coull, you there?" My words lowered to a shaken whisper, calling out to only the nearest visible hiding places that surrounded me. But all were deserted.

The image of Martha was gone. The front entrance, despite having been locked, swung open freely at the push of my hand. Having no intention to go inside, I shone the lantern quickly through the hall, my feet never once lifting from the slate doorstep. A shallow moan echoed down from the upper level, and I elevated the lantern with haste. The white light directly hit the stairway, projecting only the motioned shadow of wooden rails against the damp plastered walls.

The moan came again, much louder than before. It was a noise I'd heard many times as a child, after one of my father's heavy drinking sessions. Mumbling and groaning in his sleep, far too drunk to even awaken himself as meaningless words fell freely from his mouth.

"Coull?" I called again. "Is that you?"

No answer came, though the moaning continued, completely undisturbed by my calls. Reluctantly, I stepped inside, the lantern leading the way through the hall and up to the tight staircase.

My nerves somehow settled. Shining the light about me seemed to provide a sense of security, if not bravery to the situation. I turned back to view the grounds behind me, the hall lit up finely from below, presenting everything with a subtle shade of greyness. For a time I remained still, focusing only on the rambling moans on the upper floor. It was as I raised the lantern higher that the thin face of a distressed woman peered silently around the corner of the doorframe below me. Her eyes slowly tilted upwards to my position on the stairs, her appearance striking me with a terrible fright. My skin crawled, and my lower lip trembled. Martha Ferrell stayed still. Like a living statue, she only looked back at me, her hungry eyes hypnotising, never once straying from my own.

Jolting forward up the remaining stairs, I crashed into the landing wall as I made the sudden turn. The bedroom door swung shut with direct force behind me. With an immediate turn, the light lit up the bedroom perfectly, displaying a pale Mr Coull who sat back against the bedpost. His eyes were closed, but he himself was still in a delirious state of confusion. He continued to speak in a muttered tongue, many of his words deemed meaningless to my ear.

Standing above him, shadows struck strongly across the white wrinkled face I'd come to know so well. Without hesitation, I nudged him forcefully, placing my palm on the upper right of his chest.

"Coull!" I prompted again, alongside another gentle shake of the hand.

It took some time, but slowly his heavy eyelids opened. At first, his gaze scattered around the room, his expression dazed, vacant. He looked about himself, and it took only a moment before he glared up at the person who'd awoken him. His features displayed puzzlement at first, perhaps considering if he actually knew the figure who stood to his side at all. The aged eyes soon focused on me with familiarity and, raising a hand, he pointed a finger riddled with arthritis swiftly up in my direction.

"Ah, young Mr Wills," he stated gladly, his voice somewhat hoarse from the cold, dusty air.

I gave a reassuring smile in return, accompanied by an encouraging pat on his shoulder. Again, he looked about himself, many questions seemingly flowing through his mind before he decided to speak. He groaned.

"Eh... What happened, lad?" He sat up, manoeuvring his neck vigorously, an unpleasant crack sounding in return. "Whatever ale that was, (his accent now presenting much stronger in his confused state) ah winnae be indulging in it again, ah kin tell ye that. Where am ah, lad?"

"You're in my bedroom." I spoke the words with utter surprise of his absent-minded regard to our current situation.

"Yer bedroom?" he asked "Ye cannae do that, laddie. Nae oan the third date." He smiled, the humour now pouring through as he lifted himself upright. "Now start at the very beginning, lad." His words were gentle and calming, given the circumstance.

"I'm sorry, Mr Coull, but…but there's no time. We need to leave, and now."

Without me having to explain anything further, he swiftly nodded in agreement, accepting my words with trust, never once questioning my reasoning nor judgment. After aiding the unbalanced man towards the stairway, it took brute strength to support his weight down the narrow wooden steps, although we slowly managed and in good time, despite Coull's sudden lack of mobility.

He paused with a revelation. "She's here, isn't she?" The icy words hesitantly flew from his tense jaw, recalling the memory of what he had faced early that evening. "Go, lad, go now."

His voice spoke with extreme urgency, his temperament altering within the blink of an eye, his mobility improving drastically by the second. The door remained fully open as we reached the bottom step, the path beyond us appearing as clear as the darkness would allow. The cold air gripped us immediately, and we rushed out under the open night sky. After he managed to stagger roughly ten yards, Coull's ankle straggled, limply giving way from under him. We both fell on a small incline in the earth. A yard or so further would have seen us sheltered beneath a small tree, suitable enough to escape the fallen snow and bitter night's breeze.

Grabbing under Coull's arms with care, I tugged him desperately through the snow. A clear expression of awkwardness displayed vacantly on

Coull's face by the time I'd finished. Panting for air, I slouched beside him and placed the lantern between us.

"Now what?" I asked throughout my rapid breathing.

Coull lay flat on his back, resting his injured leg, his long white hair illuminated from the brightness of the now full moon, his facial features appearing much more elderly.

How on earth is he supposed to make it home in such a state?

I couldn't carry him, I knew that much. My heart gradually soothed its pounding, allowing my mind to steadily calm and my tense muscles to ease from the continual rush of adrenaline.

I looked over to the far land, observing the darkness of the road that was far too strenuous for Mr Coull's vulnerable state. Taking him back into the house may well be the only choice we had, if we planned on living through the night.

I knelt where he rested, hesitating on how to inform him of our current choices. Coull bolted upright from where he sat. A shaky grip rested on my shoulder for support as he stared in the opposite direction.

"Lad?"

Moving my head so as not to throw him off balance, I caught the image of the same extremely thin figure in the corner of my eye before turning swiftly and lying next to Coull. Martha Ferrell stood in the doorway of the cottage as if she had never left. Her movement slow but unnatural, it looked as though she still continued to knock on the surface of the door. The knocking noise was now much clearer than before, despite the entrance of the property remaining wide open. I went to stand, reaching for the lantern that had rolled smoothly towards our feet.

"Easy, laddie." Coull's voice slightly trembled with an identifiable worry, as I gained my posture.

We did nothing but observe the saddened figure going from door to window, from window to door. Constantly knocking. Never resting from seeking attention from within. It felt so cold now. Much colder than earlier, though we still dared not move for a time. The wind had settled to a steady breeze, allowing the sound of whimpering to be heard - the source itself unmistakably Martha.

Echoes of Home

Chapter Forty-Two

"Burn it." The words flew fluently from Coull's blue lips.

"What?" I questioned with uncertainty, my attention never once parting from the sight of Martha Ferrell.

"Burn it!" he repeated even more confidently. "Burn it to the ground, lad."

It was then the knocking halted as quickly as it had begun and Martha slowly turned her head to face us once more. We remained perfectly still, not even a twitch of movement made in her presence. Then despite the attention it would cause, Coull continued to speak in a more than convincing manner.

"What are you waiting for? Burn it, lad."

I struggled to find the words to respond, hypnotised by the eyes that looked across from me and frozen by the cold conditions assaulting my body.

"Let the torment end," Coull continued, his tone slightly louder. "How much longer must she wander around this land, this house, only to seek aid for her children that have long since passed? For an eternity she will be in torment, gaining nothing from the door at which she stands. Burn it down, lad. Set her free, and with that, let her rest."

I said nothing, only glaring mindlessly at the bleak picture in front of me. Watching her, no longer with fear, but with the purest of sympathy. A crystal tear fell freely from the eyes of her saddened face, portraying a sudden hint of beauty in her stare. An innocent beauty who had been wronged in so many ways.

A sudden sensation came over me that for a time, I didn't realise had occurred. I could feel nothing. Not the blow of the breeze nor the ice that burnt intensely between my toes. A surreal feeling to say the least. A feeling that encouraged me to believe I was no longer a part of this life but still every bit a part of this world. Not at all did I favour the thought, the idea proving only the uncertainty of my own existence.

I looked down to Coull. His posture appeared most unnatural. He lay slumped in the snow, his weary sight still focused on the house, yet his chest did not rise, his eyes blinked not at all. I almost reached the conclusion I was dead, frozen in time by the very influence of the lady who stood across from me.

Wait a second.

My gaze wandered over the view of the house. It was then I realised it appeared somewhat different to what I had come to know. The downstairs rooms were now fully alight, shining a pleasant glow through freshly cleaned glass. The sight of flickering flames could be caught from where I stood, providing me with the desirable longing for warmth and safety. Candles stood upright on the upper level windowsills, a steady flame burning at each wick. Smoke billowed in the thickest cloud from the chimney, slowly fading into the night air. To my right, a horse cart rested, almost invisible by the parading snowfall. And to the left of me, a stable building, which had long since gone. The sound of horses vacantly came from the same direction, yet the stable doors rested open, the inside presenting only frozen hay on its floor.

My eyes returned to Martha, despite her glare never once absent from mine. The knocking began again, much louder now, shortly followed by the sound of combined struggling cries. A shadow appeared from the brightness of the inner rooms. Then another, and another, until the rooms themselves seemed to be bustling with people who took great interest in seeking out the noises from the bitter night.

The candles upstairs flickered frantically as shadows passed by with haste, the noises now so loud I was almost tempted to cover my ears. But I did not. I must not. If I were to reject this spirit's cries, I was no better than the man who caused her such torment in the past.

The sensation of pure warmth suddenly tingled from my hand to wrist. I looked down to the glowing lantern of Clais Cottage, its beam still glaring an unnatural white display. The warmth continued to rise to my upper arm and shoulder, releasing the stiffened grip of the cold. Martha whimpered, her eyes now alive with tears of sorrow, though the shadows from inside never once answered her cries.

"I'll do it," I whispered promptly, my warm breath clouding the view before me.

Suddenly, every shadow abruptly halted in its place, their blackened outlines keenly watching in my direction from the safety of their sheltered rooms.

I gazed on them all with hatred, gripping the lantern more tightly with slightly numbed fingers. The rattle of the metal swung with tension as I, without hesitation, released my grip. The glowing lantern flew with grace, directly through the image of Martha and past the doorway of the house. The saddened spirit turned briefly, staring at the broken lantern that leaked out flames. Within seconds, the hall was ablaze. Smoke poured out through the open door. Martha never looked back at me but shortly after faded from sight as she watched the aggressive flames spring to life.

Before I knew it, the voice of Mr Coull again echoed through my ears, and it took him a moment, but he also bore witness to the shadow of figures inside.

"People, lad!" he yelled. "Get 'em outta there!"

He panicked after observing the quickly growing flames. Attempting to stand too quickly, he landed flat on his back. On his second attempt to regain himself, I pinned his shoulders firmly to the ground. Calling out words that he at first would never contemplate as truth, I begged him to see reason.

"See for yourself, man! They do not move, do not budge. Yet the flames grow higher and higher."

A crazed expression appeared that I could only guess was one of complete mistrust. He struggled for a time, his glare continually moving from me to the house. But soon I allowed my grip to slacken, and he watched the shadows from where he lay.

"Who…" He calmed himself to steady his breath. "Who are they?"

I did not turn back but knelt by Coull's side, who was recovering from the struggle.

"I'm not sure," I said, lifting my head to the sky. "More shadows of the past, one would guess. Only not too eager to reveal their true appearance."

"Aye, you may be right." Coull agreed with more certainty.

The heat grew stronger against my hunched back, and as I looked at the face of Mr Coull, a bright yellow and orange colour displayed vibrantly on the surface of his unblinking eyes. The ground about me heightened and dimmed with light, as though the sun were rising and setting in the space of a few seconds. Coull slouched back, more at ease with the sight before him, and although I still could not contemplate the strange series of events, I, too, lay on the ground alongside him, watching the flames spread wildly.

For a time, we forgot the cold completely. The fire had taken full control of the cottage, staining the stone walls black, flames violently pouring through the archways of the house. I looked to the shadows inside. None moved, and flames danced frantically about them. The darkened faces watched me quietly sitting exhausted on the snow.

Tilting my neck back, I allowed the heat to wash over my face. The burning cottage dominated the ground for what felt like hours, and somewhere in that time, I drifted off, my sleep once again dreamless, free from the haunted past.

Echoes of Home

Chapter Forty-Three

By the time the sun had risen, the house—or what remained of it—was identifiable only by its framed walls. The roof had collapsed during the early hours, awaking me from an unbelievably sound sleep with the most horrendous clatter. Coull somehow managed to remain completely undisturbed by the racket, lying curled on his side, exhaling deeply, as though in the deepest of sleep.

Later, help surprisingly arrived with force from the nearest lodgings, stating that the sign of smoke could not be missed through the misty morning sky. Of course, everyone who attended arrived on foot, the roads still far from safe for driving. Unfortunately, by the time they arrived, there was little to be done. What lit the sky was now nothing more than glowing embers. The unappealing stench of burning strongly wafted through the air while I wandered, creating the uncontrollable reflex to cough when attempting to speak. Shortly after, several of us helped Mr Coull sluggishly return to his unreliable feet, never once complaining about the given aid of his generous neighbours.

We said not a word to those who asked, simply explaining the living room fire, unattended the previous evening, became out of control. They took the story with somewhat raised brows, their faces showing a reluctant uncertainty to my tale.

However, I thought it best I hold my tongue temporarily on the matter. The locals of Elphin were superstitious enough. The last thing I needed was to cause caution to the few individuals who arrived willing to help.

Shortly afterwards, a young man trudged towards the house in yellow wellington boots. He carried a large leather bag over his shoulder that I soon learnt contained hot soup and tea. A most welcoming gesture, to which Coull and I showed instant gratitude.

Mr Coull stood consuming his soup, and, for a time, speaking to the faces he had known most of his life. Myself, on the other hand, sat slumped beside my now damaged car, still shaken, slurping at the steaming soup. My gaze panned over the once intimidating cottage. The shadows within had long since passed, the rooms now displaying only a gloominess to their space.

"Mr Wills?" called one of the gentlemen, whose name I was still intending to learn.

"Yes?" I returned, moving from my comfortable spot.

The man beckoned me over with a nod of his head. He was, at a guess, middle-aged with strong round shoulders that hung like canons just below his neck. A dark, full beard covered his face. And as I walked over, he stood next to Coull, nodding in agreement.

"If there is anything you can salvage, man, do it now. I've sent for my son to return with the plough. Should get through this lot without trouble. We'll have this road clean in no time.

Michael here has agreed you'll be staying with him for a time."

I looked about me, searching the faces for one that responded to the name of Michael. However, no one did. Each man stood quiet, the cold seeming not to affect them in the slightest.

"And who," I asked, my hand at the ready to point over the group of men, "is Michael?"

The small gathering of men sniggered through their teeth, truly amused by my confusion.

The bearded man continued, speaking on top of his own laughter. "Takes a generous man tae take in company. Especially when the company dunnae even know who in hell's fires ye are." His hand raised swiftly, smacking itself down on Mr Coull's tired, slumped shoulder.

I brushed off the embarrassment hastily, not wanting to cause more awkwardness toward one Michael Coull and his acquaintances.

"Aye, lad, gather what you can. If there is anything to gather at all, that is. You'll stay with me till we set things right."

It was generous of him. *Too generous*. But I refrained from showing any more gratitude than necessary in front of complete strangers.

It took a further hour for the plough to arrive and another hour on top to see the snow finally cleared from the road. There was nothing to recover of my possessions. All had gone up in smoke alongside the rest of the house, leaving me with only the clothes that hung dampened on my person. We left the site shortly after. Coull, standing alongside two men, was gently aided into a maroon-coloured vehicle, to which I followed shortly after, never once looking back.

Chapter Forty-Four

My company with Mr Coull didn't come to an end quickly. In fact, I lodged with him for some time after the burning of Elphin Cottage. It seemed to take several weeks before the tiredness ceased and I was once again able to remain awake throughout the longer spring days.

Helping Coull where I could was the least I could do. The grounds to his vast land were in need of a little upkeep, and Coull was happy for the help. And I was only too happy to oblige, spending the days of March fixing fences and rebuilding stone walls. And at the end of each day we both raised a glass to what we had accomplished.

"Slàinte Mhath," he would say merrily with a wide smile pasted across his face, his glass raised briefly to the air to match my own.

The days not spent working, we took lengthy walks through long-forgotten Highland paths, accompanied by both of Coull's obedient dogs. Coull talked and talked of the land's past as we casually ambled from one loch to the next. From Loch Cam to Veyatie, to Sionasgaig to Fionn. Filling my head with so much information, it was inevitable I'd be bound to shortly forget. That said, I didn't disturb his lectures, and to be truthful, I'd come to enjoy them.

Yes, we had become rather good friends in such a short space of time, but soon I knew only too well the time would come for me to return to Staffordshire.

During the first week of April, we decided to join some of the locals in fixing up the village's bothy. The small wooden lodging consisted of a single room with narrow bunks at either side. It was to be used by any hikers who wild-camped and trailed the rocky paths. The locals didn't find the odd tourist too much of an inconvenience, and at times, the odd sightseer provided income to some of the small businesses nearby. It was indeed heavy work, but with many hands, the job came together quickly throughout the early morning.

Many faces arrived that I had come to find familiar. Several greeted me by surname. The men who aided us the night after the fire were amongst them, although I had not formally spoken to them all for some weeks prior. I sat quietly on the rooftop of the bothy for the warmest part of the morning, replacing the stones that had fallen loose from the chimney arch. Three local children accompanied their fathers to the site at sunrise, but all had been instructed to keep themselves to the surrounding grounds and out of harm's way as best they could.

As the time hit midday, all volunteers ceased their work to engage in social natter. One of the farmer's wives paid a brief visit to the working site, delivering enough beef stew to feed us all. The men ate in silence on the green, finally wiping their plates clean with thickly sliced bread.

My sight casually panned over to Coull, who lay slouched beneath the shade of a small birch tree. There was something that didn't look at all right about him, and as I made a general nod in his direction, he gave the subtle gesture to leave in return.

Coull's health took an unexpected turn for the worst over the next few days, further delaying my long journey home. But I couldn't complain. I was in no desperate need to leave the place I'd come to think of so fondly.

That same evening, a pleasant doctor by the name of Brady called at Coull's door. Dr Brady had made the short trip from Ullapool, and despite not being local to Elphin, made the suggestion that he had made Coull's acquaintance several times prior.

Michael Coull sat at ease in the comfort of his armchair. A cigarette, as always, sat proudly between his lips. A piece of old cloth was held firmly in his hand, blotched with fresh red markings. It was then I knew the seriousness of his health, and as the doctor sighed on entry seeing Coull's appearance, he pulled the door quickly shut behind him, leaving me to pace the farmhouse hall with anticipation.

Echoes of Home

Chapter Forty-Five

C oull complained not during the final days of his life. He stayed quietly resting in the comfort of his withered chair before steadily moving to the upper quarters of his house. We'd spoken but briefly over those few days, me never wishing to cause him any further disturbance than necessary.

The two dogs sulked about the house with grief, feeling the absence of their beloved master. I took control of the property for a time, seeing to Coull's meals and much required medications, to which he showed his humble gratitude.

From the front porch, the violent sound of retching echoed through the halls, the noise always halting to a deadened silence, striking me to quickly pace towards his chambers with worry.

On my return from one of Coull's hidden paths, I spent the evening sitting next to his bedside. He had become much paler over the past several days, and tonight was no exception. Sweat poured from his brow, his long white hair sticking firmly against his pale skin. His eyes remained closed for a time, speaking to me as though attempting sleep. A sluggish chuckle flowed from his rattling lungs, and he opened his heavy eyes to peer above him.

"It's funny, lad." His throat was hoarse as he reached out for water. "I've been on my own a long time. Sometimes with only my own voice for company. Yet, as soon as life starts to pick up, it's time for me to leave."

"You aren't going anywhere," I said to comfort him, collecting the glass from his weakened grasp.

Coull shook his head wearily, disagreeing with my statement on point. "Aye... Aye, I am, lad." He spoke in a calm confident tone. "Always wondered what it would feel like, that sensation of exiting this world. And now...now I have that very feeling." Coughing abruptly before sinking his head back into the feather pillow, he continued.

"It's all ma own doing, of course. But now the time has inevitably come. Well... I can't help thinking it'd be nice to have a little longer."

He turned his head towards me and gave a slight smile. The remark he made, I took as the purest compliment. As I placed my hand reassuringly on his clammy arm, Coull rested himself for a second.

Breathing deeply, I observed his tightened chest struggling to rise then quickly collapsing.

"Les!" he said, startled from his rest, his tone mellowing as he continued to quietly speak.

"A letter... There's a letter for you over there, lad."

He lay pointing towards a chest of drawers on the far side of the room.

The surface of the counter lay covered in many papers that had without doubt piled up over the years. At first, it was difficult to determine the paper he suggested, though the envelope soon came to light as it fell from among the gathered documents. The thick brown envelope was fairly new in comparison to the other faded items, the back presenting a red wax seal that had been freshly stamped.

I gently waved the sealed envelope in the direction of the resting figure. He gave a small nod of approval in return, beckoning me to the seat from which I came.

"It is not for now." His breathing worsened with every word he attempted to voice. "Open it when the time is right, lad."

I nodded agreement in a way he could visually acknowledge my nonverbal response. Then, with ease, I slowly returned my hand back to his upper arm.

"Rest for now," I said convincingly.

Coull's head slowly fell to face the nearest wall.

Holding back my emotion was more difficult than I expected. My eyes suddenly blurred. The forming tears welled up before me, and I sat watching over my sickened friend. I soon stood, allowing Coull to rest through the night ahead, and made my way towards the landing. Coull's voice called out again, though much softer than ever before.

"Les?"

I turned sharply, staring at the huddled shape that lay motionless against the wall.

"I'm here," I called out through the faded light.

"Thank you, lad… Thank you for everything."

*

The funeral took place some days later and, in some way, I felt as though I had ended a journey the same way it had begun. The morning was bright as I walked down the narrow road towards the service. The mountains beyond displayed a vibrant green with patches of tinted brown now that all the snow had come to pass. The sky showed only a small cluster of white clouds amongst the endless blue, and the breeze of the forenoon air flew warmly across my face.

I was unsure exactly in what direction I was headed. A small group of people dressed formally in black gathered outside the small local café. Their faces, although emotional, appeared pleasant enough upon my approach. A few of them recognised me from the previous weeks, whispering to those unaware of my connection to Coull. My appearance was somewhat scruffy, owing to the fact I hadn't been able to acquire a suit in time for the occasion.

Regardless, I took it upon myself to shake the hands of all, enquiring if I could accompany them to the burial site. They appeared somewhat happy enough with the thought, and before long, they made tracks. I followed to the rear of the line. Not a word was uttered until the road levelled, the trodden ground much more suitable for walking than before. Two by two, they crossed the quiet road, leading us to a small black gate, barracked by tall trees at either side. I had never come to notice such an entrance prior to this, and as I tailed the small group from behind, a wall of trees blocked out the blueness from above.

It was a beautiful place. A place that felt in some way secret to any outsider. The scent of freshly cut grass wafted about the grounds, providing the true sensation that spring was in the air. The warmth of the sun graciously beamed down, its shine gleaming on the coffin's surface and onto the neighbouring headstones.

The service was short although respectable in many ways. One by one, a flower from each of the guests was dropped on the lowered coffin. Each person repeated a small prayer, stepping back to line where they'd stood. I didn't move for a time, thinking only of the man who had, in some ways, become a father figure to me over those winter months. And as the service ended in song, gradually the lingering party dispersed from the open grave. And then so did I, leaving Mr Coull reunited once more with his family. To rest forevermore.

Turning away, my head hung low, I urged myself to fight away the emotional tears that fell from my saddened expression. My shoes nestled softly into the freshly cut grass as I sulked away from the rectangular hole in the ground. And to help ease my mind from the sorrowful moment, I read aloud the scattered line of headstones on my passing.

"Ian MacDonald. Catharine Campbell. Susan Daily. M Sulli…"

My reading abruptly halted, and I retraced the trodden grass back to the previous stone, my brain trying desperately to recall where I'd heard such a name before. My eyes sharpened directly to the stone surface as I silently read the inscription.

Susan Daily
Of Loch Borralan House
Born 1942 – Died 20/02/1997

My heart struck like thunder within my breast, as the engraved name spoke aloud to me from a memory long since passed. *It can't be…* I thought, while rereading the bold chiselled font embedded in stone. Both hands clutched tightly within my pockets, unwilling to loosen from the cause of such a surreal view. My glare remained focused, until the sight of the next headstone again caught my eye. "Oh… Oh god." The names now jumped out at me without a thought from which they came.

M. Sullivan
Beloved Husband of
J. Sullivan
Born 1917 – Died 20/02/1997
Also
J. Sullivan
Wife of the above.
Born 1910 – Died 20/02/1997

My stomach clenched while I strongly held back the longing to heave. I dragged myself over to the next stone with a sense of dizziness, yet denied myself the right to faint. Its shape and font was an exact replica of its neighbouring stones. And although now expected, its writing forced my trembling knees to buckle, sending me quickly kneeling to the ground.

James McCabe.
Husband of
Margaret McCabe
Born 1953 – Died 20/02/1997
And
Margaret McCabe
Wife of the above.
Born 1960 – Died 20/02/1997
Also
Bridget McCabe
Daughter of the above
Born 1988 – Died 20/02/1997

My increased breathing slowly eased in time, though the lingering nausea struggled to fade from my unsettled gut. I observed the three headstones, fear and disbelief clouding my thoughts. I remained still, studying the writings that felt to be more dreamlike than reality, until a voice projected from behind.

"Born to live and then to fade, left forgotten in a shady grave."

I turned immediately to the comforting voice of such a dark telling rhyme. I remembered her smile instantly. The young waitress from the café walked toward me, dressed fully in black, her pale skin shimmering from beneath the sunlight.

"Pardon me?"

"Oh… It's nothing," she said quickly, brushing off the subject. "Just something my mother used to say."

"Running a little late?"

"No, I never arrive early at these things. I prefer to say my final goodbye alone, it's much more meaningful this way."

"I see." I slowly panned my head back down to the graves before me.

"Did you know them?" Her tone suddenly transformed into that of sympathy.

I said nothing for the moment, unsure if my words would emerge as truth or lie.

"Tragic really wasn't it? she continued. "I was only a young girl myself but recall people talking about it the next morning. Comes to something when you're unsafe in your village. I can't wait to get outta this remote dive, gonnae move to the city one day, I hope."

"Talk about what?" My state of mind was now truly confused by the woman's insistent natter.

"Why, The storm of ninety-seven, of course. The poor souls took shelter at an abandoned inn farther up road. Unfortunately, the storm lasted some days, came out of nowhere, too. By the time anyone could reach the inn, they all had long since perished."

My eyes tightened to a close, remembering so vividly the very people whose names now lay etched in limestone. I sat back, the panic becoming visibly present to the girl who stared kindly down at me.

"Are you quite all right sir?" Her voice now fell to nothing but a shallow whisper as she knelt beside me.

"Yes, I just need... I just need a minute, please."

"You live in the old Elphin cottage, don't you?" she continued while bending forward to observe my current state.

"Not many newcomers tend to hack that old place. The last guy, only a short time ago fled in a hurry, after receiving some rather urgent news. Found his car totalled off the main road, they did. Had to cart his body all the way to Inverness. Such a shame, really nice guy, too. He'd visited the café a couple of times during his stay."

Although my thoughts were elsewhere, I glanced upward to the woman who towered over me. The sun momentarily blocked by her bunched-up hair.

"Do you remember the name?" I asked, still looking up at her smile.

"Of the man?... Sure, I believe it was Jonathan."

Echoes of Home

Chapter Forty-Six

I locked the black gate on my leave. The day quickly grew warmer by the hour. The heated air in the distance expanded, giving rise to a shimmering heat haze. I walked alone for a time, down the narrow road and across a stagnant spring, with only my thoughts to console me. The hills and valleys about me sang out with life. The few animals that presented themselves basked in the long-awaited heat, never once disturbing as I came into view. But although the sights were glorious to behold and the weather most splendid, I had come to witness a sensation of stalking loneliness following closely over my shoulder. It was a sensation I'd come to know well since my arrival at Elphin. A feeling I thought had all but passed.

With my coat soon tied to my waist, I paced towards the inclined curve of the Highland road. Sweat spotted intermittently across my forehead, and I thought of the long journey home to Staffordshire. A true plan was not set in place, though I had the money to see me home in time.

The trip would take me casually from town to town, until a rail line route became available to fit my needs.

I wish I didn't have to leave.

The thought continuously lingered during the scheduling of my complex travel plans, but just as this secluded place began to feel like home, it was indeed time to put its beauty behind me.

The road soon straightened out, displaying an endless path ahead. And for the first time since my stay, several cars sped past me at rapid speed, their radios blaring out music I'd not yet come to know. It may have been due to the fact I was deep in thought. Or that I'd not realised where I stood without the grounds layered in endless snow. But after I looked back at my trodden steps, the Iron gates of Elphin Cottage towered to one side, and to the other, the small lodging of Clais.

The sun gleamed down on its shadowed stone, providing a peaceful impression in the distance. I took some steps back, too curious to identify the remains of Elphin in full light.

It had only been some weeks, still I'd forgotten the true length of the cottage's entrance. The loose gravel that could send a person falling, as it did me once before, loudly crunched beneath my feet. I recalled falling that day, misplacing my phone and looking up over to the distant cottage.

Should I look back? No... No, best not. There is nothing left to see.

The thought vanished in an instant.

I turned the bend, and Elphin Cottage came into view. An uncontrollable shudder flew sharply down my spine, from neck to tailbone. Reminiscing on the events that took place skipped my heartbeat. With the windows now smashed and the doors burnt to nothing but ash, the interior of the vacant space was clear for all to see. Resting in the tall grass beneath the shade of an old apple tree, I gazed at the scorched stones. It felt pleasing to escape from the sun for a time, and as I dropped my coat on the uncut lawn, a smooth brown envelope protruded from its inner pocket.

I held it upright, admiring the wax seal pressed into its flap that clearly marked the letter C. Now seemed as good a time as any to ready myself for what Coull wished to say. And as I slowly lifted the lip of the folded card, the wax satisfyingly snapped, revealing a dozen folded papers.

Dear Leslie Wills,

I would like to think that over such a short period of time, you and I have unexpectedly become the closest of friends. It was a friendship, however, that neither of us wished to seek, but without doubt, a friendship we both so desperately needed.

Living alone for such a period caused great stubbornness in my life, and it wasn't until I heard that my time would evidently come that I greatly feared passing alone.

You alone, Mr Wills, without knowing, put an end to that much-hidden fear. And with that, I give you my most meaningful thanks.

As I may have already made clear, I have no remaining family. No children, siblings, parents, nor spouse. No one I have depended on or been reliable for, for that matter. I am a man of little wealth, who has not the interest nor desire to chase such a thing during this lifetime. My home and land are my kingdom, and in truth, the only things I hold dear to my heart. The memories of my family are seen through my ageing eyes as I walk the rooms of the house, longing to turn back the wheel of time.

I do believe that one day, what I write will come of some sense. But it will serve you well to take note. Do not live as I have. Settle, and live your life to the fullest, never to be always wishing you lived in the past. The past will never change. It remains still in your mind, until the image begins to haze with your last longing breath.

If you will accept, I have enclosed the necessary ownership papers of my property. I wish for you to inherit such items, but on one condition. That both my dogs will be taken care of when I go. Other than that, I have no requests. You may do as you wish, with me knowing I have left what matters most in the best of hands.

And finally. The events that took place at Elphin Cottage should now finally be put to rest. My weakened bones shake at what I witnessed when the world went black that night. A lady standing above me as I lay slumped to the icy ground, her pale skin shining in the crisp moonlight. It was a spirit who had sought only the help of others for many years. And that very same spirit who aided me to the house that night before your arrival. I never mentioned such a thing before, almost second-guessing whether such an incident indeed occurred. But it did. And I must tell the one person who would believe it before the thought is lost forever.

That being said, Elphin Cottage now stands a smouldering shadow of its former self. A ruined symbol of humanity's much worser times. Not just for Elphin but throughout this small island we call home.

Please find reassurance as you read this letter, Mr Wills. As the days and weeks have passed, I have spent many a night rattling my brain in regards to what we saw that night. And every night, without doubt, I reach the very same satisfying conclusion. Martha Ferrell should now be able to finally rest.

Yours truly,
Coull

A lump swelled, lingering deep within my throat, that for a time made it difficult to even breathe. Folding the letter with care, I held it firmly in both hands, contemplating the gift and the comforting idea of remaining here at Elphin.

The tree above me swayed from left to right with the first breeze of the day, and as I stood, I looked once more towards the destroyed building. With a sudden movement of the neck, a shining reflection caught my eye from the distant grass. I made my way towards the sun-mirrored spark and knelt to the ground, placing one hand on the golden memorial plate that had been unaffected by the aggressive flames of the house.

I translated its final line quietly for the last time.

"In time, forgive our sin."

A sound of child's laughter carried its way faintly through the humid air, directing my sight to the location of Clais Cottage. The air made a motioning wave through the sun's heat, and I peered up to the hill's crest. And for the shortest of moments, I caught a glimpse of a sight that presented no trickery but the innocent shape of two young girls. Children, playing beside the falling walls, the sound that followed them heard only as joy and none of despair.

The laughter faded shortly after that, the movement of air deteriorated their existence from clear view. Blinking in protest to the dryness, I reluctantly gazed down until the sensation had come to pass. My watch immediately caught my attention as its hands began to move. I watched the seconds tick by and held the watch to my ear, listening to the workings of the inner cogs.

Its mechanism sounded so much stronger than I had ever heard. I smiled down at my wrist, gracefully stroking the glass face with the tip of my finger. I looked about me with a sense of ease.

The sun had peaked its highest. Even the branches of the trees whistled in calming song to the steady breeze of the day. And as I stood, mesmerised by the surface of the loch and clouds that peaked the mountainsides, for the very first time since my arrival, Elphin no longer felt frozen in time.

Dedicated to all those who fell victim to
The Great Famine 1845-1849
&
The Highland Famine 1846-1856

About the Book

I always felt a great fondness for the Scottish Highlands. It may be the rugged scenery, or the engrossing history. But it is without question, the last true slice of wilderness that remains on our small island.

I visited the small village of Elphin several times throughout the years, partaking in wild camps and kayaking trips. Each time, the one sensation that always struck me was how isolated its land would make me feel. An adventurous hike through the Sutherland estate would always provide me with the sense of being the only soul left on earth. And coming from the area of Stoke-on-Trent, that feeling is hard to come by.

The house title of Clais is very much true. In the spring of 2016, I took another trip to Elphin and eagerly paddled off on my kayak into the Sutherland estate for five days. When writing this book, I tried at most to picture the scenery, the unbelievable vastness and rocky landscape of this particular trip. It was on the second day that we were unable to continue boating, due to the aggressive weather. We stopped, making up camp for the evening, and by pure coincidence came across a cottage ruin, huddled secretly between two hillsides. A stream gushed rapidly past its front, as we made our way to its entrance. Its roof had completely collapsed, but we sat inside to shelter ourselves from the cold regardless. I remember being mesmerised not only by what the history of this small cottage possibly held, but the lonesome location in which it had sat empty for many years. It was a fascinating spot for a story.

For a long time, I have had a great interest in studying genealogy. So much so, that all of the characters within this story are named after my ancestors. Martha Ferrell, the main topic of this book, was the name of my three times great grandmother. And very much like the story, in reality, she died in 1845, during the first year of the Irish Famine, along with her two young daughters. All, devastatingly, perishing from the result of undernourishment and exposure. Martha's only son, Peter Coull, would soon after travel over to Scotland via cattle cart with his father, where he would remain. If he hadn't, I would not be here today. The character of Peter Daily, although again a family name, was very much created for the book. However, his class of character strongly mimics the cruelty and selfishness that many landlords inflicted towards their farming tenants during this time, despite their very few needs.

Although I was willing, the idea of setting this particular tale in the location of Cork, Ireland, felt a little too close to home. The Great Hunger that began in 1845 is a topic that, although both inhumane and unjustifiable, is a subject of shared knowledge. It was while studying the tragedy of such horrendous events that my attention drifted over to Scotland and how the Potato Blight and crop failures in Ireland soon began to impact the lands and farmers of the Scottish Highlanders. It was at that point I looked back on my accidental visit to Clais cottage, the setting and location so fitting for the story I wished to respectfully tell. And once completed, I hoped in some way it would reflect how the unfortunate had to cope in order to survive.

The location of Clais Cottage can be found on the outskirts of lochan na claise within the Sutherland Estate.

Acknowledgements

Thank you to my wife Emma, and my children, Brandon and Meredith, for providing me with the time and support to write this book, despite it sometimes eating into our family life.

To Jim Ody. If it wasn't for your guidance and support, this book would not be in the position it is today. A big thank you, for putting up with my inexperience in the wide world of writing and granting your friendship along the way.

Thank you to Question Mark Press Publisher, for taking me on, getting my book out there, and providing the time and support I truly needed. I'll try my best to keep the pages flowing.

To Sue Scott, thank you for the thorough proofreading of this book, not forgetting your well received advice.

To Emmy Ellis, thank you for your help & marvellous cover talent.

A big thank you to all the BETA readers and ARC readers, who dedicated their time to work through this book.

About the Author

New Author to QMP.

Born and bred in the county of Staffordshire, Matt is a keen reader of classical, horror and fantasy literature and enjoys writing in the style of traditional ghost stories. During his working life, Matt joined the ambulance service in 2009, transporting critically ill patients all over the UK. After writing his first novel, Matt was welcomed into the family of Question Mark Press publishing and now dedicates his time on future releases. His hobbies include genealogy and hiking, and he enjoys spending time with his wife, Emma, his children, and his family.

Connect with M. L. Rayner

Facebook: www.facebook.com/MLRayner

Amazon Author: www.amazon.co.uk/M.-L.-Rayner/e/B08LTXNSH4/

Goodreads:
www.goodreads.com/author/show/20902655.M_L_Rayner

Question Mark Press:
www.facebook.com/QuestionMarkPress

Instagram: https://www.instagram.com/m.l.rayner/

Email:
Matt_rayner43@hotmail.com
Questionmarkpress@gmail.com

More Available QMP Titles

*The place that never existed

*Lost Connections

*A life time ago

*Come back home

*Mystery Island

*Beneath the Whispers

*Little Miss Evil

*A Cold Retreat

amazon.com

kindle
unlimited

goodreads

audible